The Moondial

Hans Hergot

Bezzle Books
Columbia, South Carolina

Bezzle Books
1492 Lake Murray Boulevard
Columbia, South Carolina 29212

This is a work of fiction. Names, characters, places, and incidents are a product of the author's imagination. Locales and public names are sometimes used for atmospheric purposes. Any resemblance to actual people, living or dead, or to businesses, companies, events, institutions, or locales is completely coincidental.

Ordering Information:

Quantity sales. Special discounts are available on quantity purchases by corporations, associations, and others. For details, contact the "Special Sales Department" at the address above.

The Moondial / Hans Hergot. — 1st print ed.

ISBN 978-0-9894565-2-4

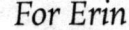
For Erin

The World of Hurt

THE YELLOW ISLES DANYFYR THE WASTES GRIFFTON

THE WASTES

ICE BRIDGE

TO ROLLY'S CAMP

● FIRST MEETING

● ICE CAVES

THE GLACIERS

● LUFTALL CLIFF

● YUNAUT VILLAGE

● ROLLY'S SHIP

THE NORTH SEA

Chapter 1

The glitter of gold caught Hranna's eye. The reflection of the sun off of metal was the only thing brighter than the snow-covered landscape surrounding her. She was drawn to the golden glint the way a fish is lured-in by a painted piece of bone.

Hranna shifted her weight, sending a subtle signal to the two skisen that pulled her sled. Sensing her will, the woolly beasts turned toward the point in the distance where Hranna thought she'd spied treasure.

Her hunt had been a failure. She'd been on the ice a whole ten-day without success, travelling over the ice bridge into the far stretches of the snowy wastes. Now, it looked as though she might not leave the ice empty-handed. Metal was more valuable than a luftall's hide anyway.

A few moments later, Hranna stepped off the sled. A snow drift separated her from the metallic shine she'd seen across the ice. The peaks of blue glaciers marked the horizon. Snow covered the landscape in every direction. Her village lay a day's ride away. Hranna was completely cut off, beyond reach of help or rescue. She would have to approach cautiously. No one alive would leave metal to rust in the snow, and no one alive would let such a precious possession go without a fight.

Her skisen looked to her for instructions. She put a hand parallel to the ground and moved it slowly downward. Wait, she told them. Though there was nothing to lash them to, Hranna trusted them not to move. Her skisen, Nar and Bin, were well trained.

She walked past them up the snow drift, running a mittened hand over Nar's curved horn as she passed. The big male stamped impatiently. The heart of the team, he was always thinking with his belly, hoping she would untie them so they could forage. Hranna needed them ready in case there was danger.

Her feet sunk into the loose snow as she crested the ridge of the drift. She slipped her bone-handled knife out of its tanned sheath. The handle was beautifully carved from a luftall's hind tusk. She gripped the handle even tighter, feeling its smooth contours through her animal-skin mittens. She remembered the fat beast the tusk had come from. It had been her first kill and the knife a reward.

If the handle of the knife was nice, the metal blade attached to it was priceless. It was a tool fit for a chief's son. Her father, the chief of her village, had only Hranna.

Hranna's thoughts drifted toward her father and her village. In all likelihood, Inoah would be the next chief. Her father was ailing. He might die that very season. Hard as the thought was, Hranna had to think of her own future. She wondered whether Inoah would marry her. If he didn't see her as a wife, he might see her as a threat to his reign.

While the women in her tribe could, by rights, kill a man who tried to take them against their wishes, Hranna's situation was perfectly reversed. If Inoah didn't take her, it would mean her death.

Hranna let these thoughts drift into the background as she focused on the task at hand. She was hunting the precious piece of metal now as intensely as she tracked a luftall swimming under the ice. There was no past or future, only the present. It was what she loved about hunting.

Hranna crouched as she neared the top of the snow drift, peering cautiously over the crest.

She blinked and put a hand to her eyes, momentarily blinded. Sunlight reflected off the metal, bouncing directly into her eyes. It took a moment for her vision to adjust and another for Hranna to comprehend what she saw.

On the opposite bank sat a strangely dressed man. He wore no animal skin. His smooth clothes were a uniform blue. In his outstretched hand sat the shiny metal object. Behind him, a small hole opened into the bank of the snow drift, as though he had improvised the kind of burrow a wollen might build. Despite the cold, the man was sitting still. It was a bad sign for him but a good sign for Hranna. If he was dead, she might pick over him like a luftall carcass. She might even crawl into the hole to see if it held more treasures. As for the man, she would let the snow give him a proper burial.

Hranna approached a little more boldly. The metal that she had seen from afar sat in the man's outstretched hand, glittering like the morning star. Snow had already formed a light dusting over his clothing. No one could survive such exposure, but the man had a strange look to him. From under his hood, what was visible of his face was covered by fur as thick as a browen's. The men from her village had smooth skin.

Hranna began to wonder whether this was really a man at all or whether it was a demon. Demons had been known to mate with browens—the big, hairy beasts that roamed the ice. A man might not sit so still and live, Hranna thought, but a demon might. And a half-demon, half-browen certainly could. Hranna crouched instinctively as she approached the seated creature. She held her blade at the ready.

Were it not for the shiny piece of metal sitting so lightly in the man's outstretched hand, Hranna would have followed her instincts and fled. But she was so close. Hranna did not know what the object was, but she saw what it could be. With such a pretty piece of metal for a dowry, Hranna might buy her way into Inoah's heart.

If he did not marry her, he was sure to have her killed or banished from the village to preserve his legacy. A chief's daughter could not be suffered to remain.

If banished, Hranna thought she might survive on the ice. She was a gifted hunter. But such a life would be almost worse than a quick death. It took a village to truly live. When her father died, if she were not Inoah's bride, she would be finished.

Hranna moved slowly, toe to heel, as she approached the seated figure. She was close now; close to the object; close to securing her future. She could see it more clearly: round, smooth, and polished, with odd etchings running around the casing. She checked her grip on the knife, releasing and tightening each finger in sequence.

The man was not moving. The wind overhead sent a wave of powdered snow over the side of the drift. Down in the shallow valley that sheltered Hranna and the seated man, all was silent and still, save for Hranna's rising breath and her hand as she reached for the metal.

Hranna touched the object. It fell to the ground. Her mind seized up, wondering what she'd done to displace the metal object. Even as her eyes tracked its descent, a hand closed over her left wrist. Hranna reacted on instinct. Her knife sliced through the air toward the man's throat. He pulled her trapped arm over, blocking the angle of the blade. She nearly stabbed her own forearm.

Hranna reversed the blade, bringing it back toward the knuckles that held her wrist. She risked cutting her own arm. The man, sensing her intent, released her wrist, catching her knife-hand as she followed through on the strike. He twisted down on her thumb causing her to drop the blade. In the same instant his free hand caught hers. They were locked together. Even sitting, the man was nearly as tall as Hranna.

"Lasdef!" The man spoke. Hranna couldn't understand him. She lashed out with her knees. The man turned sideways, accepting the blows but not the intent behind them.

"Havek." He was speaking again, calmly, as though they were dancing together around the fire rather than locked in a mortal struggle.

Hranna shifted her feet to kick out. The man jerked her hands upward, throwing her off balance. Simultaneously he extended both legs in a scissor motion, catching her behind the knee with one heel and trapping the top of her foot with the other. Hranna went to her knees. The man twisted her wrists backwards, pressing his thumbs into the top of her hands. Her elbows folded in on her sides. She couldn't move her arms or her legs. She saw her knife, just a step away, but totally useless for all that. Hranna gazed fiercely into the stranger's icy blue eyes.

"Stop," the man said.

Hranna gasped. The shock of hearing the demon-man speaking her language momentarily took the fight out of her. He must have noted her response.

"I need your help, please."

He released her arms. Hranna jumped backwards, landing on the balls of her feet. Her eyes moved toward the knife that had been a gift from her father.

The man's gaze followed hers.

"Take it," he said. In a swift motion, he reached down, retrieving his metal object and tossing the knife toward her. It stuck point-down in front of Hranna's feet. She plucked it out of the snow, brandishing it in front of her.

The man held his arms open wide as if inviting Hranna to hurl the knife through his heart.

"You're a Yunaut," he said. "You must be. The language you speak, it took me a second. It's very close to Kamau, which I know quite well—"

"What are you?" Hranna demanded.

The man smiled. His broad teeth were nearly as white as snow. "I'm an explorer." He stood up slowly, obviously not wanting to startle her. He brushed the snow off of his clothes without leaving so much as a drop of water. "A man from far away."

Hranna's mouth fell open. Her poor fabric would have soaked up water, spelling nearly instant death, were it not for the animal skins coverings that separated her from the cold. This creature who called himself a man had a demon's tricks.

Hranna backed up one step, then another. She measured the man's legs, anticipating the lead she would need to regain the sled.

"Don't go."

"Why not?"

"I need your help."

How could a man whose coat shook off the snow like a skisen's need her help? Hranna hesitated. The glare of sunlight off metal hit her eyes again.

"I used it to signal you across the ice." The man was wiggling the round, metal object, causing the light to dart across her face. More aggravating was the mischievous smile on his face.

"You like it?" he asked.

"What is it?"

"A moondial."

Hranna shook her head. She didn't recognize the term.

"It shows me the right way."

"Ha!" Hranna hadn't meant to let the rough barking laugh escape her lips. The man was obviously lost.

He shrugged and looked at the moondial. "It tells directions by the moon or by the top of the world. But I'm on the top of the world now, and I haven't seen the moon in months."

Hranna didn't know what he meant by the world. She considered the snowy wastes, the coast, and the scrub forest to be the whole of creation. Sometimes an object appeared in trade that put her beliefs to the test, like the metal knife she now handled. But Hranna lacked the imagination to consider such matters. Usually a hunt was sufficient remedy against such musings. However, what Hranna lacked in imagination or worldly trivia, she made up for in knowledge about the moon's cycles. What else would a hunter know better than the moon under which she prowled?

"The moon hides her face," Hranna said. "You will not see her again for—" she paused to count on her mittened fingers, feeling them move as she numbered the remaining days, "twenty days."

"Hmm." The man nodded. He looked up at the sky the way a husband looks at a cheating spouse. "Then my people are at your mercy."

Hranna crouched low again looking for an ambush. She scanned the sides of the surrounding snow banks. She saw no one, but if they were anything like this man, they might lay undetected, buried in the snow.

"They are not here. They are several days away." The man reached into the hole behind him and pulled out a pack, which he slung over one shoulder.

Hranna heard the tell-tale tinkle of metal. She looked at the pack. Hanging from strings on each side was a village-worth of wealth. The stranger carried riches beyond imagine nonchalantly on his back.

If only she had found him frozen to death, she would have had enough wealth that she might rule the village with or without Inoah. He might be the chief, but her word would be law.

That such an arrangement had never existed in her world did not stop Hranna from envisioning it. For one with such a limited imagination she was infinitely practical. On a hunt, when facing danger, she improvised. Her mind became just as flexible now, as she examined the burnished metal sticks hanging from the blue man's pack.

He must have interpreted her silence as an agreement to help. He began to relate his story. Hranna only understood parts of it. Her mind was on her own future, not his past.

"We started north too late. The boat we came in got trapped in the ice. There were eight of us. One of the passengers, Doctor Martin, would love to have met you," he digressed. "I went for help. I was heading toward our station—it's like our village—then the moon disappeared. If I don't return with supplies in about seven days, they'll starve." He tilted his head sharply to the side as if everything had been thoroughly explained. He appeared to be waiting on a response.

She could track him, she thought. Wait till he dropped dead of exposure and then collect his metal. It might be a long hunt but well worth the effort. Yet, the thought rankled her sense of honor.

"Maybe if you took me to your village, I could trade for supplies?"

"No." She said it automatically. Her village was only one day away—though the concept of day and night had less meaning when the sun was always up as it was now. Hranna felt the passage of time as a thing in her bones, as instinctive as breathing.

She could not take him to her village. There was no telling what her father would do if she brought a stranger to the village or if he yet had the strength to manage such a situation. He might trade with the stranger or kill him. No matter what happened, Hranna would get no share of the wealth. It would be spread among the village as were all spoils of war or found treasures. Everyone prospered when a luftall corpse washed up on shore. Hranna would be in no better position than she was now. That was unaccept-able.

"They would kill you." She told a half-lie. They might kill him. Probably not. Hranna nervously wiped away condensation that had formed on the top of her lips. Her hand went to the notch on her disfigured ear. She wondered if her lie was as transparent as it felt. She shifted her feet side to side to stave off the cold that was seeping into her skin through her furs. To stand idly on the ice was to die.

The man did not move. There must be something magical about his clothing, Hranna decided.

The blue man was smiling at her again. She didn't know what he found so amusing about the situation that he would smile, especially if he needed her help. Weren't his people suffering? Weren't they at her mercy? Hranna set her feet like his and stared at him. She sniffed.

"We hunt," she said.

His smile faded.

"All the supplies you need, food and oil, the luftall has."

The man held his hands up half apologetically, "I don't know how."

Hranna sheathed her knife and hunkered down onto her haunches. It was time to trade.

The man mirrored her movement. She was glad that he knew how to haggle. They squatted, facing each other. "I will teach you. For a price."

"What price?"

Hranna had leverage. He needed her help. But she was in a precarious position. Without his metal she would remain alive only so long as her father lived.

"The moondale."

"Moondial." He corrected her.

Hranna bit her lip. "The moondial, and the metal from your backpack."

"No."

Hranna stood up, dusting off the front of her knees. She turned to go.

"Wait."

Hranna stopped. She turned back. He remained hunkered. She resumed the position.

"I cannot give you the moondial. It belonged to my grandfather and my father and one day, if I live to have one, my son."

It was a sentiment she could understand. Her hand slipped over the bone handle of her knife.

"I can give you the metal on my pack and twice as much metal when we return to my camp with a luftall. It's the metal you want, right?"

Hranna made no indication, positive or negative. She sat for a long, cold moment.

"Done," she said and stood.

The man stood as well. He advanced toward her with his hand outstretched. Hranna took a few steps back. She examined his hand. Each finger had its own small pouch, unlike her mittened hands. She stared at his glove in amazement.

"And a pair of your gloves," she blurted. It was wrong to alter the deal after agreeing, but she had to try.

The man stood with his hand still extended. His smile returned. "Agreed."

Hranna did not know what he meant by the gesture. She extended her hand as he did, still several strides away. A gulf separated them. The man crossed it in two quick steps. He took her hand in his before she could move. He was close enough for her to see green specks in his blue eyes and to feel the steam off his breath. He smelled like a freshly cut tree from the scrub forest.

"My name is Rolly."

"Hrolly," she repeated.

He did not correct her pronunciation.

He released her hand. "Let's hunt."

Hranna stumbled a little as she backpedaled up the snow drift, heading toward the sled. Rolly followed her easily up the incline. His boots sunk deep in the loose snow.

Her skisen snorted as they approached. The beasts had been long idle in the snow, though such was hardly a problem for creatures with such fluffy, white fur. She put a hand on Nar's horn. He might cause trouble around a stranger.

She heard Rolly crunch down the slope toward them. She thought of the hunt. His heavy footfall would alert every luftall in the area. The luftall swam under the ice. Normally Hranna relied on her silent sled and the muffled, padded feet of her skisen team. She would track a luftall till the ice grew thin. Then she would harpoon it through the ice using a short spear made from a curved skisen horn and connected to a rope. Her skisen would then pull on the rope till it broke or till the luftall wearied from the exertion and loss of blood. When it grew tired and desperate, the luftall would burst through the ice. The hunter had to avoid the fore-tusk and the hind tusks, slicing at its unprotected neck. With the skisen's help, a hunt took more courage than physical strength.

Hranna shook her head. Such a hunt would never work with Rolly at her side. Together, they could not move fast enough to track the luftall under the ice, if one was stupid enough to stick around after hearing Rolly's heavy tread. They would have to hunt luftall in the open, a thing unheard of even for a seasoned hunter like Hranna. It was dangerous beyond belief. Only the desperate or the foolish would attempt it. Hranna was desperate and the metal fortune on Rolly's pack made her a little foolish.

"Are these—how do you call them?" Rolly pointed toward Nar and Bin.

"Skisen." Hranna provided the word.

"They're magnificent."

Rolly moved toward Bin, the smaller female. The animals were skittish, nervous about the stranger's presence and smell. Hranna scented it too, the smell of fresh-cut wood. They probably wouldn't spear him though—probably. But, if they did, thought Hranna, she could more easily take his metal. She stepped aside, curious to see what happened.

The man pulled off one of his magical five-fingered gloves. He offered a bare palm to Bin, placing it just in front of her nose. Hranna almost nodded in approval. She checked herself. She had to admit that Rolly knew his way around animals.

He patted Bin's soft neck. She acceded to his touch. He scratched behind her ears. Rolly had just made a friend for life.

"She's beautiful."

"How do you know it's a girl?"

Rolly didn't pause in his thorough ruffling of Bin's fur. He answered with his back turned. "Because of the straight horn. Unlike this one—" He offered his hand for Nar's inspection. Nar snorted.

Rolly ran a hand up Nar's curved horn. Hranna was surprised the old skisen accepted Rolly so readily.

"My team of explorers, we study this place and its creatures. You see, when they mate, the male's curved horn allows it to lock with the female's—"

"I know what it does." Hranna interrupted him.

Rolly turned back to her with a sheepish grin. "Sorry, when I start explaining something it's hard to stop. It's a bad habit of mine."

"What do you mean, study?" Hranna's curiosity got the better of her.

Rolly considered. "We learn about this place. For instance, my friend Amy Martin, she would love to talk to you about your village, your way of life."

"Is there any other way of life?" Something about the way he talked rankled Hranna, as if the villagers were less than people to him. Also, his mention of Amy, his female friend, bothered her in a way she couldn't explain. Hranna certainly did not intend to talk to that woman.

Rolly brushed off her brusque response. He was looking past her. "There are many ways of life where we come from. Green mountains and meadows. Cities and steam engines."

Hranna did not know half of the words he was using. It sounded like magic.

Rolly fixed her with his blue eyes. They were brighter than they had been earlier, if that were possible. "Haven't you ever wanted to know why the sun rises? Why the moon hides?"

The ideas hurt her head. Hranna waived them away as if they were snow flies. "If you want to learn something. Learn to hunt."

Rolly's grin increased. "I can't wait."

"Good. First lesson: follow me."

Hranna mounted her sled and put her weight to the balls of her feet. Her skisen felt the shift and began moving forward. She did not lean back. They quickened their pace accordingly. She would show Rolly how sorely he was lacking on the ice. It was her turn to smile now, looking back over her shoulder at the rapidly disappearing figure.

Only he wasn't disappearing. Rolly was easily keeping pace with his long legs. He wasn't even jogging, just maintaining a fast walk. His legs snapped smartly forward. His stride was long, not as long as it might have been. She could tell he was trading long strides for short, speedy steps. Her eyebrows scrunched. Her smile faded.

His beamed out through his face-fur.

Hranna finally slackened her pace. It would not do to tire her animals just to make a point. And if she had to face a luftall on the ice, she might need Rolly's help as well.

Hranna took up a flagon full of luftall oil and pressed it to her lips. She felt the lukewarm, salty liquid slide down her throat. It burned her stomach, causing a warm glow to spread through her limbs. The man looked at her.

She tossed him the flagon. He caught it in stride.

She watched as Rolly took a swig. He pulled a face. Hranna grinned.

Rolly tried to wipe the coagulated fat and gristle off his tongue. Hranna scolded him. "It's good for you," she said, just as her father had told Hranna on their first hunt together.

Rolly stopped pawing at his mouth, seeming to accept the inevitable. Hranna kept watching. When he looked at his fingers, she knew that the luftall fat had affected him too. Perhaps he wasn't a demon or a browen after all.

"It's like alcohol," he said.

"Like what?"

"A liquid we drink. It makes us feel funny."

Hranna nodded. There were men who boiled the luftall fat and captured the spirit of the luftall in a bowl. It was a powerful drink.

They rested at midday. The term had little meaning in the always-sunny sky. Without the movement of the heavens to tell time, Hranna trusted her instincts. She let the skisen forage. Rolly examined her sled.

"What's this?" He touched a curved skisen horn that was lashed to the sled.

It was the weapon she used to hunt luftall: the horn of a male skisen hafted to a foreshaft by a cord of sinews. The foreshaft was then attached to a short, stout pole. In a pinch, the foreshaft could be replaced easily allowing the hunt to continue. She held a second skisen horn in reserve for just such an occasion.

"It's for spearing the luftall." She took it out and demonstrated a thrust at the ice. "The curved horn hooks the luftall like a mating skisen."

She thought she saw Rolly blush a little at the call-back to his earlier gaffe, but it was hard to tell through his face-fur.

Rolly took the weapon out of her hand. She was loathe to relinquish it to a man she still didn't quite trust. Finally, she relented.

He acted as though there had never been an awkward pause. "Wouldn't it be better to have a longer pole or a weapon you could throw from a distance?"

Rolly obviously knew nothing of hunting luftall through the ice. However, for their current assignment, confronting a luftall in the open, he might be right.

There was nothing to be done about it now. There was no wood available nearby with which to construct a suitable spear. Their village location had been chosen for its proximity to coastal fishing and to the brush forest that provided her stout pole and foreshaft. There was nothing like it on the open ice.

Hranna did not for an instant consider tipping the pole with her knife and hurling it. She would rather charge a luftall head-on, a prospect she'd been seriously entertaining since they started out that morning, rather than risk losing the precious knife her father had given her. Like Rolly, she too hoped to pass it on to her future son, who she hoped would be a chief in his day.

She shook the fantasy from her mind like snow off her hood. Inoah would be chief and she would likely be dead. Even if their crazy venture succeeded, should

Inoah choose another—Hranna's hand went to the nick in her ear where a luftall's tusk had taken off a solid chunk of cartilage—Hranna would at best be the richest woman in the village. Her son would never be chief. Not unless she started her own village. The idea came to her as bright as the morning star that sometimes pierced through even the ever-sunny sky. Were such a thing possible? Could she form a new village if she succeeded?

Hranna watched as Rolly handled the hafted weapon. He wasn't as awkward as she expected him to be for his height and weight. But he was obviously no expert either. It didn't help that the weapon was not balanced for fighting but was weighted for its utilitarian purpose—busting through thin ice and impaling a luftall behind its breathing hole.

The clumsy weapon was not built for hunting on the open ice for the simple reason that no sane hunter would attack the huge, three-tusked beasts in that manner. Only the fear of losing her position and her life prompted Hranna to do so now.

Rolly had no idea what she was getting him into. She almost felt bad for him. Hranna found it strange how sharing a hunt with a person could change one's opinion of them so drastically. Earlier, Hranna had willed Rolly to be frozen dead. It was hard to conjure the same wish once she knew his name and they had shared a flagon of luftall oil.

The trouble was, Rolly thought Hranna knew what she was doing. She had no clue how to even go about hunting a luftall out in the open.

That didn't bother Hranna much. On a hunt, she improvised. She felt that, when facing the luftall, she would know what to do. The hunt was in her bones and in her blood for generations. Weren't there tales of famous hunters who fought an enraged luftall on the ice? Hadn't they succeeded?

No. Now that she thought about it, most of the songs were about how they killed the luftall and were themselves killed by mortal wounds received in the struggle. But what could one expect to arise out of such a harsh, cold life except ballads of tragic heroism? In their stories, no one emerged unscathed.

Hranna gulped down another swallow of luftall oil and let the slow, crawling burn spread through her limbs, providing her some comfort.

She whistled softly to the skisen. Though they had roamed far over the snow, they raced back. Before stepping onto her sled, Hranna secured the skisen and the weapon.

Drinking the luftall oil had given her courage. Tomorrow she would face the beast. She would not wait to have her fate decided by Inoah. She would live or die by her own hand, based on skill and luck.

***

They trekked all day through the barren wastes of a snowy landscape that changed only in its contours not in contrast, as the sun never rose or set. Hranna noted landmarks as they went: a jutting rock where she and her father had weathered out a storm, a field of thin ice through which she's pierced a big luftall, one with gray fur.

Soon enough, Hranna's sensitive nose picked out a change in the air: a bright smell, salty like luftall oil, light as the air. They were nearing the ocean and the cliffs and caves of the luftall. Hranna picked out a promontory on the horizon that signaled where the cliffs began. She shifted her weight on the sled. Her skisen, Nar and Bin, obeyed her subtle prompt. They changed direction, moving toward the outcropping. Rolly walked along beside them.

Hranna drove the sled into the dell of a snowdrift still a short distance away from the cliff. Her internal sense of time told her that night had fallen. They should rest before attempting the impossible. She unhitched Nar and Bin. They waited patiently for her command. Hranna flicked her hand forward. Nar snorted and led Bin off to graze on whatever shrubbery they could find buried just under the snow. Hranna unstrapped her tent and unrolled it on the ice. The ends of the thick animal skin flapped in the gentle, evening breeze. Hranna's nose itched at the cold wind.

Untying the long, curved ribs of a luftall from the sled, she staked them into the snow, pressing with all her weight. They sank slowly into the ice. She twisted left and right to encourage their descent. Once Hranna was convinced that they were firmly erected, she artfully arranged another tanned leather skin over the tips of the luftall ribs. She checked over the surface of the tent, lashing the top to the base with thin, sinewy thread. If she accidentally left a large enough hole, she would never wake from her frozen slumber. Finally, she took a roll of skisen fur from the sled. The roll was thin, but, when unwound, the fine fur expanded to form a fluffy sleeping pad and matching blanket. She had cut it perfectly to line the bottom of the tent.

Rolly had other plans. Hranna watched as he pulled a metal tool from the side of his pack. It unfolded like an elbow till it was long and straight. Its end was flat and at least two hands wide. He dug its metal tip into the side of the snow bank.

It scooped ice even better than a wollen's sharp paws. Hranna surmised that he was building a burrow similar to the one she'd found him beside earlier that day. It was an interesting technique, something she placed in the back of her mind against necessity should she find herself alone and exposed on the snow at night. Of course, she didn't have that wonderful metal digging tool. But maybe she would receive it when the hunt was over. If they succeeded, he had promised her all the metal that hung from his pack and more.

Hranna checked her narrow tent once more for holes. The top was covered from patches where she had made minor repairs. The tent had character, she thought.

Hranna looked over at Rolly. He had gone into his wollen hole. Snow was issuing from the hole where he was excavating his cave. She was glad that he didn't expect to spend the night in her tent. It was tight enough as it was, but with two? Her hand reached for the notch in her scarred ear.

***

She had to give Rolly credit. He had maintained a steady pace all day and had not complained. Neither had he wasted breath on idle conversation. Although he obviously had questions, he had the good sense to keep them to himself. She looked at him now. He was seated in front of his hole as he had been that morning, tinkering with his precious moondial. Rolly shoved the round, metal cylinder into a pocket on his blue jacket.

Hranna, meanwhile, had pulled a bowl out of the tent. She'd fashioned it from a luftall skull. She fed some oil into its base. Working the back of her knife against a rough, black stone, Hranna sent a spark into the bowl. The luftall oil ate the small spark and belched out a flame. Hranna had been ready for the sudden fire, but its warmth and light still delighted her. She watched as the oil settled into a slow burn at the bottom of the bowl. Though there was no darkness to ward off, the little flame was still a comfort to her.

Rolly walked over and joined Hranna, hunkering back on his ankles just as she was doing, though she knew that his clothing would allow him to sit in the snow without consequence, unlike her rough animal skin. She was aware of what poor stuff it was next to his magical fabric. Suddenly ill at ease, Hranna put a hand to the side of her head, instinctively covering her ear.

"That's a neat trick." Rolly nodded toward the flaming skull.

Hranna shrugged.

She pulled a rough grill out of her tent. It had been fashioned from the bones of a large fish. Placing it over the bowl, she reached into a pouch at her waist, removing a handful of dried meat. Technically, she could eat it cold. But like everything, it tasted better warm.

Rolly also reached into a pocket and pulled out yet another magical object. It was bound in animal skin. Hranna had never seen such fine work. He opened it. Its flesh had been sliced into hundreds of pieces that were as thin as snowflakes. Hranna tried not to stare as Rolly took a stick from his pocket and began scratching away.

"It's called a 'book.'"

"Buk." Hranna repeated.

Rolly smiled. "I use it to remember my thoughts." He showed her his handiwork. Hranna could discern lines of scribbles that looked like they'd been made with the end of a burnt stick, but much smaller and neater.

"We call it 'writing,'" he explained. "We make our words into signs or pictures."

Hranna, as the daughter of a chief, immediately grasped the implications. Her people had drawings. They painted on bones or on animal skin. But they had nothing so fine as the feathery stuff Rolly was writing on. Nor did they know how to capture their words. What possibilities would be open to them if they could match Rolly's skill?

As with Rolly's improvised snow cave, Hranna saved the idea of writing in her mind. It was useful knowledge, but only if they survived the dangerous hunt that loomed over their heads like the cliffs just a short walk away.

"See this?" Rolly showed her the book again. On it was a rough drawing of the rocky outcropping that had sheltered Hranna and her father against the storm. It was a good likeness, Hranna thought.

"I've been keeping track of landmarks since I left my crew. That way I can use point-of-sight navigation to get back to them even without the moondial." Rolly nodded to the big pocket on the front of his jacket where he kept the strange object. "Always have a backup."

Hranna's eyes returned to the cooking meat. She didn't know what he meant by navigating. She found her way based on instinct and the lessons her father had taught her about the ice.

Rolly continued moving his stick across the book, looking occasionally at Hranna in a way that made her slightly self-conscious. Hranna found herself reaching up toward her ear. She arrested the movement, refusing to let her discomfort show.

She divided the meat evenly between them. They each swallowed a mouthful of luftall oil as well. Finally, Hranna removed a second luftall skull from the tent. She scooped snow into it and set it over the flame, reducing the icy mix to water.

Hranna took a sip. It tasted good after drinking salty luftall oil all day. She handed the bowl to Rolly. The body needed water to survive, but to eat snow directly would cause one to get too cold. Only those already near death were foolish enough to shovel snow into their mouths.

"Thank you," he said. His hand closed over hers momentarily as he received the bowl. It felt as though a spark from her fire-starter had touched her fingers. Hranna withdrew her hand. She was careful to avoid his hand when he returned the bowl. He might be a demon after all, to cause such sensations with a simple touch.

With a final flourish of his stick, Rolly pulled at his book, ripping a piece from it. It was so thin, she thought it would surely melt as soon as she touched it. She did not possess magical gloves like Rolly. Yet the sheet did not melt. She examined what Rolly had drawn. She could see the small flame from the burning luftall oil dancing behind the drawing.

Looking back at her from the sheet Rolly handed to Hranna was a face. It looked just like her mother. Hranna gasped. How did the demon-man know what her mother looked like? She had been dead so many years.

"It's you," he said.

Hranna had never seen her own face clearly. She looked at the drawing's chin and touched her own chin. She looked at the ear. A piece was missing. She touched her injured ear, where the luftall tusk had grazed her head leaving a scar under her hairline and taking a triangular piece of cartilage with it. She looked up at Rolly with widening eyes.

"Take it," he said, indicating with his hands that she should roll it up. Hranna complied. She tucked the drawing into the fold of her furry jacket.

"Thank you."

Abruptly, Hranna bent down and blew out the flame. She carried the bowl and the grill away from the tent. She drank the remaining luftall oil. Her father had taught Hranna never to waste food. It had a bitter taste, and the sensation it sent through her limbs had been weakened by burning it. She scrubbed the fish-bone grill and the bowl with loose snow, cleaning them as best she could.

When she returned to the campsite, Rolly was nowhere in sight. He must have crawled into his wollen hole for the night. Hranna hoped none of the furry, fanged beasts decided to crawl in after him.

Hranna slipped into her tent and curled up. She closed her eyes against the ever-bright night, but sleep was a long time in coming. Something about

Rolly's gift made her uncomfortable—or if not the drawing, then the man who made it.

Hranna could easily clear her mind on a hunt. However, the quiet of a long, arctic night gave her too much time to think.

She took out the drawing and examined it again. Her mother had been beautiful. The woman looking back at Hranna, the supposed likeness of herself, was also pretty. Hranna had never know that about herself. Certainly her father had told her often enough, but she had seen how even an ugly child might be loved by a kind parent.

The woman in the picture looked noble and brave, much more so than Hranna felt. Replacing the image in the fold of her jacket, Hranna closed her eyes, imagining for the hundredth time how she would attack the luftall on the open ice. She would dart past its long fore-tusk, avoiding the hind tusks, and score a blow on its exposed neck. She hoped that if she envisioned the scenario enough, the thing itself might come to pass. But if that were true, then what of her other vision: of being impaled, a horn sticking through her stomach, raising her into the air, as she looked into the hate-filled eyes of a luftall?

Hranna started as the tent flap opened. Her hand went to the bone handle of her knife.

Bin was standing at the foot of the tent. The smaller of the two skisen had raised the side of the tent with her straight horn and was patiently awaiting entrance. Hranna smiled. She motioned with her thumb, giving

Bin the sign to kneel. Hranna did not want to repair yet another hole from the skisen's straight horn. Bin obeyed the hand signal. She crawled into the tent on her knees. Hranna fell asleep peacefully nestled in the skisen's warm, white fur.

Chapter 2

Hranna jerked upright in her tent. Her hand flew to her chest. She searched frantically for the luftall tusk that had skewered her. She found nothing. She had been dreaming. It had been a nightmare. Bin nuzzled her hand gently. Hranna returned the gesture, patting the skisen on the head, assuring her everything was all right. Except it wasn't. Everything was far from all right. She was about to attempt something that was the stuff of legend.

As the false fear from the bad dream seeped out of her limbs, Hranna felt other promptings from her body. She scrambled out of the tent. Even legends had to attend to simple functions.

On returning to the tent, Hranna went about her morning ritual. She rubbed a bit of luftall oil on her hands and face before replacing her mittens for the coming day. She'd been in too much of a hurry to don them earlier. She ran a rough, oil-covered finger over her black, arching eyebrows, then over the notch in her ear.

Unlike the other girls in the village, Hranna had never cared about her looks. She was the chief's daughter. She had a strong arm and could pierce a luftall's tough hide through the ice. Until last night, she had thought that a worthy enough measure. But she wondered whether Rolly would care about such skills. This led to an uncomfortable thought as to whether the men in her village, who could hunt just as well as her, assessed value in the same way that she did. They seemed to like the preening young girls in the village. Hranna angrily rubbed the remaining oil into her hands before putting on the mittens.

The protective sheen that the luftall oil provided was all the hygiene that the rigors of a hunt allowed. Not everyone could smell as fresh as a new-cut tree. Hranna was thinking again of Rolly. He had been in her dream as well, though she could not recall what part he'd played.

Bin slid out of the tent and joined Hranna on the ice. She examined the structure before folding it up. Bin had torn a hole in the side with her horn that would need patching. Hranna didn't blame Bin this time. Her abrupt awakening from the nightmare must have startled Bin too. Besides, the lovable skisen had kept her warm during the night.

Hranna whistled for Nar. She heard his response from over the ridge of the snowdrift. Rolly emerged from his hole at the sound of her whistle. He came out head-first, followed by broad shoulders. She didn't see how they fit through such a small hole.

Hranna took out a simple bone needle and some sinew. She sewed up the hole that Bin had made in her tent during the night. It really needed a more thorough patch, but it would do in a pinch. She didn't know why she was fixing it, just out of habit maybe, considering that she might never need it again. Or maybe she was fixing it to keep her mind off the coming hunt.

She broke the tent into its component parts and stashed it on the sled. She hitched Nar and Bin to the sled before giving the creatures a going over with her eyes and her mittened hands. She examined their horns and their padded hooves. By the time she returned Bin's last hoof to the ice, Rolly had his pack on his shoulders, ready to go. He gave her an easy smile.

Hranna scowled back at him. She'd felt a challenge in his friendly grin.

She turned away from Rolly and focused on checking her hunting pole. It stood upright, tied to the handle of her sled. She checked the sinews that attached the foreshaft to the pole and also the sinews that hafted the curved skisen tusk to the foreshaft. After assuring herself that the rig was tight, Hranna removed the second foreshaft from beneath the tent. She attached it to a belt at her waist opposite her knife. She was as ready as she could be.

"Can I help?" Rolly asked.

"Can you?" Hranna shot back. She mounted the sled. "Today I bring you the luftall. You give me the metal on your pack, twice over?"

Rolly nodded.

She shifted her weight, willing the skisen toward the neighboring cliffs. Rolly followed.

On arriving, Hranna unhitched the skisen. She would only need them if she succeeded. If she died, she wanted them to be free to roam the ice in search of food. Perhaps they would return to her father. Riderless skisen were known to occasionally do that.

Before leaving the sled, she put a rope of braided sinews over her shoulder, thinking it might come in handy. Her mind stepped again through the deadly dance with the luftall's tusks. This time, she envisioned herself putting her knife in the beast's eye socket. It was a satisfying daydream, and like many such dreams, totally unrealistic. More likely the luftall's fore-tusk would pierce through the back of her skull. At least that would be a quick death, thought Hranna, compared to wasting away on the ice after being exiled by the new chief Inoah.

Hranna shoved the thought aside. On the hunt there was no room for such considerations. And this hunt promised to be more intense than any other. The prospect sent a chill of excitement up her spine that had nothing to do with their icy surroundings.

Hranna stepped to the edge of the cliff. The ocean covered the horizon, its foamy caps sprouting like an old man's hair. Her father had told her that somewhere out in the ocean was her mother's soul. Hranna was glad that her mother was close. It meant that

Hranna would not have to travel far to join her should she fall to the luftall's tusk.

Looking directly down the face of the cliff was a bit dizzying. There below them, on rocky ledges that stuck like tongues out of the gaping cave openings, lay a dozen or more luftall. They were long creatures, fat in the middle, covered all over in brown fur, and possessing danger on both ends. Three tusks bristled on their faces: a long one where their nose should be and a shorter tusk on either side of their mouth. The powerful tail in the back could crush a person to death.

She turned to climb down.

"Wait." Rolly touched her arm. She shrugged off his touch. If he interrupted her like this on the hunt, she'd be dead.

He looked serious for once. "If they smell us coming, the game is up."

Hranna addressed him with defiance, "Do I stink?"

She hunted luftall that swam under the ice and had never considered the importance of smell. Hranna knew that the wollen's nose was sharp and that a hunter had to be wise to get near one. Yet she did not want Rolly to know that she had no idea what she was doing hunting luftall out in the open.

Rolly held up the moondial. "We all stink to the animals. Don't your skisen know your smell?"

Hranna conceded the point, though she was at a loss as to how they would mask their scent.

Rolly attached the thinnest piece of metal to the top of the moondial. A small rod on its base fit into a correspondingly small hole on the moondial's face. Hranna did not know it was even possible to craft metal so delicately. He held the moondial over his head. This simple gesture put it at twice her height. It disoriented Hranna that anyone could reach so high unassisted. She looked to the snow for stability.

He brought the device back down to his chest and showed her.

"The wind is aimed back toward our camp," he said.

Hranna watched the thin metal piece flutter in the breeze.

"Like this." He blew across the top of the moondial. The metal flag matched the direction of his breath.

"Try it."

Hranna blew. The small metal flag shifted accordingly.

Rolly bent down and picked up a handful of loose snow. He tossed it into the air. It flew in the direction the moondial had first indicated. Hranna raised one eyebrow.

"A backup test, just to be safe," he said. "Okay, I don't think they'll smell us coming."

Hranna climbed down the face of the cliff. Rolly waited till she had gained a ledge before he followed. She appreciated the gesture. If he dislodged a stone, she didn't want it to knock her in the head. As he was climbing down, Hranna spotted a likely enough beast.

On a long ledge, level with the ocean, lounged a young, male luftall. His tusks were just starting to show.

If she had to face a luftall, Hranna had no visions of glory about facing a giant bull male in his prime. She would do what the wollen did in the wild—strike at the weak. Even such a young luftall would provide plenty of meat and oil for Rolly's people to survive on. And if their meat grew thin, perhaps they would trade for more metal. Hranna did not seek honor from this hunt, only survival and profit, which, in her situation, were one and the same.

While Rolly was still halfway up the cliff, Hranna made her move. She wanted full credit for the hunt, and she didn't fully trust his skills. Certainly he had strength and guile. After all, he had trapped her with the moondial yesterday. But this was a luftall hunt.

Hranna tied the end of her rope to a rock jutting out of the cliff. She used it to assist her descent to the luftall's ledge. Then, attaching the other end of the rope to her hunting pole in the traditional manner, Hranna stalked the young luftall. The beast lounged comfortably and unconcerned. Only a hrall, a great fish of the ocean, could challenge it at sea. And only the browen could take a luftall out of the ocean. A browen could never descend the cliff. The luftall felt safe. Though it sensed her presence, the animal moved only enough to fix Hranna with a glassy eye.

She lunged at its back. The cub, finally recognizing danger, snapped sideways, aiming a hind tusk at

Hranna's chest. But Hranna had the advantage of surprise. She stuck the curved skisen horn deep in to the cub's right flank, twisting it on impact. Without ice to impede its initial strike, the weapon sunk deep into the luftall's flesh. The short pole slipped out of her hands, disappearing into the luftall's fatty side. The creature bellowed in pain and rage.

It rolled toward Hranna, trying to crush her. She scrambled over its body but was not quick enough. Her ankle got trapped between the rope still attached to the pole and the animal's flank. The luftall continued to roll, dropping off the ledge and into the ocean. Hranna felt herself being pulled with it. She twisted her leg, grabbing hold of the cliff. She felt the full weight of the skisen, then heard her ankle pop. Pain seared up her leg.

The beast dropped into the sea. Hranna hung from the ledge. She willed her body to pull itself up onto the ledge. Her arms were not responding. The splash from the luftall when it hit the water washed over her. She was freezing. Her leg felt like it was on fire.

She felt a pair of hands on her shoulders, dragging her onto the ledge. She looked up into Rolly's blue eyes. He had the same look that her father wore when she did something stupid and dangerous.

Sitting on the ledge, Hranna looked down at her leg. The bone was broken clean through. Her foot was dangling from a ligament like a piece of bait. She couldn't comprehend the sight. It was like the limb belonged to someone else and only the pain belonged to her. She watched as Rolly loosened his belt and looped it around her calf. His face was grim.

Hranna saw the hunting rope twitch. The luftall was still attached. When it was tired and desperate, it would turn to fight. She pulled the knife out of her belt and rolled onto her hands and knees. The pain was beyond reckoning. Rolly shoved her roughly onto her back. Her mind swam, and her spirit yearned to join her mother in the afterlife of the ocean.

"Don't move."

"The luftall."

The luftall broke through the surface of the ocean, landing at the end of the long ledge, sending a huge spray into the air. It was too soon, Hranna thought, and the beast looked too big.

She realized that it was not the young male that she had attacked. It was much larger and female. It was the luftall cub's mother. Rolly fell back at the sight. Hranna raised her knife. She saw the beast's lowered horn and thought of her death in the dream. The luftall reared, preparing to plunge down on Hranna and Rolly, to crush them or spear them or both.

A falling star streaked through the sky over Hranna's head. The flaming red star hit the raised luftall in the chest. The smell of charred luftall fur mixed with the creature's desperate cry. The enraged beast slid off of the ledge and back into the ocean. Hranna could make no sense of it.

She looked back at Rolly. He was still sitting on his backside. In his hand was a smoking cylinder as red as the fallen star. It was more of his demon-magic. Rolly must have summoned the star. He dropped the smoking metal and crawled over to Hranna. He took the knife gently out of her hand.

"This is going to hurt."

Rolly cut a piece of leather off the bottom of her jacket and placed it into her mouth. He bent over her injured leg.

The pain increased, if such a thing were possible. It radiated from her ankle, up through her back and into her shoulders. She tried to move, but Rolly threw the weight of his body across her thighs. She saw him toss something into the ocean and realized it was her foot. Her mind swam in and out of consciousness. Wherever she went, the pain followed.

Rolly took a pouch from his backpack. He applied a powder as fine as snow to her leg stump. He took a small metal cylinder out of his pack and pressed it to her arm. She felt a pinching pain, but it was nothing compared to her leg.

"Hrolly."

"I'm sorry. I couldn't save your leg. I gave you something for the pain."

"The luftall—"

"We didn't get it."

"—is coming."

Hranna saw the line attached to the cliff go slack. Some part of her mind knew what that meant, even if Rolly did not.

Again the ocean ripped apart. It tore in half like a piece of wet cloth. The injured cub landed on the ledge, bellowing a challenge. Rolly turned to face it with Hranna's knife in his hand, its blade still covered in her blood.

Still on her back, Hranna turned her head to witness the final part of their saga. Had anyone been there to see it, she had no doubt their song would have been sung forever. She felt the wet, rough ledge under her check as she turned to watch. She brushed a strand of stray, wet hair out of her eyes.

Rolly was brave and protective of her. He did not allow the beast to come near Hranna but rushed it. He had her knife in one hand and his digging tool in the other. He clacked the pieces of metal together and screamed at the beast, no doubt hoping to scare it off. The luftall was not running, thought Hranna. He had tried to run. It had turned to fight.

As he closed with the beast, Rolly feinted to the left; the beast snapped its long fore-tusk in that direction. It hit only air. Rolly had spun at the last moment, closing within striking distance of the luftall's head.

The hind tusks, Hranna thought, just as one blossomed out the back of Rolly's left shoulder. The digging tool fell out of his limp hand. It clattered to the ledge and fell into the ocean. Hranna mourned the loss of metal. Blood ran out of Rolly's shoulder, staining his blue jacket.

Rolly still held the knife. Though he was stuck to the luftall by the tusk, he fought on. Rolly plunged the knife into the luftall's neck, stabbing it over and over. The beast rolled and took Rolly with it. He could not avoid the roll as he was still pinned to its tusk. Yet the weight of its head alone was not enough to crush him. He continued stabbing the beast's neck.

Slice it, thought Hranna.

As though he had heard her thoughts, Rolly ceased jabbing and brought the blade across the neck, severing the supply of blood to the beast's brain. Gore spurted out. The beast slumped to the ground. The pole in its ribs, the repeated stabbings, and the final slash at the neck had finally accomplished the improbable. They had killed a luftall on the open ice. Hranna smiled as she fell unconscious. She felt her mother's soul calling sweetly to her from the ocean nearby.

Chapter 3

Hranna saw fire. This wasn't supposed to happen. Her soul should have joined her mother's in the deep, blue sea. What wrong could she have committed to go to the place of eternal fire where no snow fell? Her mind supplied ready offenses to condemn her. She had disobeyed her father. She had murdered her mother. She had cheated on Inoah with a strange man. Hranna struggled with the accusations. No. They weren't true. Her father lived. She had never married Inoah. She recognized the phantom nightmares as a dream. Caught between waking and sleeping, Hranna blinked. Her eyes fluttered. The fire remained. It, at least, was real. Hranna breathed deeply. She still lived. As clarity returned to her mind, so did the pain.

Hranna looked down at her leg. She couldn't see it. It was covered in the furs from her sled. Hranna struggled onto an elbow. The fire was just an arm's length away. It was the low burn of luftall oil gathered in a small hole in the rock. Hranna looked around.

She was inside a cave. The ceiling was damp but she was not wet.

Rolly's shadow blotted out the narrow entrance to the cave.

He knelt by her side.

"Drink this." He handed her a small metal pouch full of liquid. Was there no end to his treasures?

"You lost a lot of blood. This will give you some nourishment." He showed her how to twist a lid to get at its contents. "And I need you to drink as much water as you can stand. I filled your flagon with plain water. When you finish it, I'll refill it."

"What happened?" Rolly's arm was in an improvised sling. His jacket was stained red with blood, but the hole where the luftall's tusk punctured his arm and the fabric was patched with a white material that looked like a spider web.

Hranna's knife hung at his waist. She looked at it with alarm, feeling a pang of covetousness. She let the emotion pass. He had killed the luftall with it and perhaps still had need of it.

His eyes tracked hers. He handed the knife back, offering her the hilt. She slipped it into the sheath at her waist.

"I hauled you up to this cave. It's above the high tide. Not too wet." Rolly crouched by the fire. He took off his glove and warmed his hand. "I harvested this luftall oil from the beast below. And I used your rope to pull the rest of it to the top of the cliff, piece by piece. I had to do it before the tide came in."

Hranna knew the amount of work involved in field dressing an animal as big as a luftall. She couldn't imagine doing it one handed and down on the cliff. Had he slept or rested since the hunt and the nasty wound he'd received? In answer to her unspoken question, Rolly sat down heavily.

Apparently he had not.

"I've got to sleep now." He slumped over onto the rock beside the fire, pulling his glove back on and his hood up over his head. He took a thin blanket out of his bag and slipped it over his legs the way one puts a hook through a worm.

"The sled is loaded." His head nodded. She thought he might have fallen asleep. "If I don't wake up, follow the drawings in my book back to my crew. They'll give you all the metal you want."

As she drank the liquid from the metal pouch, a deeper sense of thirst erupted in her throat. She took the flagon and drank half of it. She wanted to drink it all but decided to keep some back against her thirst. She would drink it in sips as her thirst mounted. She did not want to wake Rolly to ask him to get her more water.

Hranna sat up now. It felt weird doing so, since she was missing a foot. The stump of her leg dragged over the blanket, causing the pain to increase. She pulled back the tent and the fur blankets. Under her knee she could see Rolly's blue belt still wrapped around the top of her calf. Below that she could see nothing. Her foot was gone. Rolly had wrapped the remaining stump in a white gauze that matched the spider webbing on his shoulder.

She looked at Rolly's face as he slept. Hranna hadn't thought he could hunt a luftall under the ice, much less on top of it. She had underestimated the hairy stranger. In the small cave, over the smell of burning luftall oil, she could still smell the scent of cut trees. It comforted her, reminding her of the village beside the shrub forest and of her father and of the smell of a newly-made sled.

Hranna did not know how much time had passed since the luftall attacked. Her internal sense of time was not working. Perhaps it had resided in one of her missing toes? That she could joke about the serious injury gave Hranna a sense of calm. Rolly had said that he'd harvested the luftall before high tide. So she had slept at least half a day. It might be morning of the next day.

Hranna settled on her back. The cave was dry and warm, almost too warm. She was no longer thirsty or particularly hungry. Besides the pain, it would have been a pleasant campsite. They should stay here a few days to recover, but she knew Rolly's people were suffering, waiting for him to return. He had said that if he didn't return soon, they would starve. Between a one legged hunter and a one armed, blue giant, they would have to make their way back across the ice with the luftall. If she was going to live through the next day or two, she needed rest. With all the practicality born of a lifetime spent hunting luftall on the ice, Hranna closed her eyes and fell instantly asleep.

Chapter 4

Hranna stood on the ledge with the rope tied around her waist. It had been Rolly's idea. He intended to use the sled to haul her to the top of the cliff. Hranna didn't know how he convinced Nar and Bin to assist him. She had explained how to drive the sled using one's weight. He had stopped her, explaining that the sled was already weighed down with luftall flesh and oil. It couldn't carry his weight and pull her up. It was a lucky thing the skisen were pulling downhill. Otherwise, Hranna doubted the skisen could have pulled her extra weight up the face of the cliff.

So, instead, Hranna had taught Rolly a few hand signals, though she never believed her skisen would allow him to lash them to the sled.

She had been wrong. Apparently the first impression he'd made on Nar and Bin had been overwhelmingly positive. Now she was attached to the rope, which was itself tied to the sled, which was hitched to the skisen. Hranna felt three tugs on the rope. She braced herself for the ascent.

The rope grew tight around her chest. Hranna began traveling upwards slowly. She used her hands and her good leg to keep her injured stump from hitting the cliff. Once at the top, she pulled herself over the edge and pushed herself to stand on one foot. It would never do to rest in the snow even for an instant. Rolly left the sled and walked back to her.

She looked at the sled. It was loaded nearly beyond capacity with luftall.

"We'll have to leave some of the luftall behind so you can ride," said Rolly.

They had already had the same discussion several times that morning.

Hranna spoke up defiantly, "I can take care of myself."

"But my crew can't. We'll reach them sooner if you ride."

"And what if you starve because of the food we leave behind?"

Rolly examined the sled with a critical eye. The runners were already bowed under the weight of the parts of the luftall that he was able to salvage. It must have cost him a great deal to haul all that meat to the top of the cliff with his injured shoulder. To leave any of the precious cargo behind seemed to cause him as much pain as the luftall's tusk had exacted.

"I can strap it to my back with the rope."

"Its blood would seep even through your magic fabric." She had told him this many times. Guarded as he was from the elements by his clothing, he could not see the impracticality of his plan. Hranna, who had grown up on the frozen wastes, knew how deadly any liquid could be. It was a minor miracle that they had survived the wetting they received while attacking the luftall. Had Rolly not had the good sense to dry them out by building a fire out of the luftall's belly fat, they would not have lived through the night.

"I could strap you to my back," he said. It was a new suggestion. Hranna considered his proposal. It would be hard on her pride, but she was nothing if not practical. She would not be deadweight like the luftall flesh. And she could help hold herself on his back, giving some relief to his injured shoulder.

Hranna nodded her assent. Rolly slid his fancy backpack off his shoulders and added it to her gear on the sled. Having her belongings commingled with another's had not happened since her aged father had been strong enough to hunt. Hranna didn't know how to feel about it.

Rolly wrapped the corded rope around her thighs and over her waist in a complicated pattern. He then repeated the loops, making circles around his shoulders. She realized that he was rigging a complicated harness.

"If we had some wood, I could build a sled and pull you."

"Like a skisen?" Hranna flashed a smile that was wasted on Rolly's back as he moved toward her so that she could mount.

"I'm sure Nar would teach me a few tricks."

Hranna threw her arms around his shoulders, grabbing the front of the rope harness that crisscrossed his chest. She gripped his waist between her legs. He grabbed her good leg under the thigh. Her bad leg stuck useless in front of him. His lame arm could not grasp it. She felt him shudder with pain as she adjusted her seat.

"Okay. I'm on." Up close, the smell of cut trees overwhelmed Hranna's senses. She resisted the strong desire to bury her face in the back of his blue hood.

Rolly, who could not sense her inner struggle and who likely would have laughed at her if he had, tightened the harness.

"Did you take any bones from the luftall?" Hranna restarted the conversation hoping to distract Rolly from any pain her weight was causing to his shoulder and to distract herself from the urge to smell him and from the waves of discomfort that rolled up her injured leg with every jolting step. Even though the snow cushioned his footfalls, Hranna felt each one.

"I didn't have a cutting tool," he answered. "But I did take one souvenir—" His voice drifted off. His mind had obviously turned in on itself. Perhaps, having felt how much she weighed, he was reconsidering his plan to carry her across the wastes.

Hranna left Rolly alone with his thoughts. She had plans of her own to make. She considered her options as they walked. First, she had to survive her injury. Such major wounds often began to stink after a time. If that happened, then an inner fire would spread through her body, consuming her soul from within, killing her.

But if her leg healed, and she hoped Rolly's powdery medicine might help, then she would take the metal from Rolly's camp and return to her village.

Hranna began to feel a glimmer of hope, as bright as the morning star. She began to hope that she might survive this impossible hunt and return to her village as the richest person alive. She shook off images of returning to the village a cripple. She told herself that the deformity would add to the allure and mystery to her new fortune. No one could say that she hadn't earned it.

If Rolly's promise held true, she would never have to work again, though she knew that a life of idleness would drive her crazy. She could still hunt; even with one leg she was sure that she could find a way, especially if she had enough metal to fashion a weapon that would kill a wounded luftall without requiring her to close with the beast.

She would use her free time to create a way for her people to record their words just like Rolly. It was a noble pursuit and one that recommended itself to her practical side. Of course, being able to read and write might also serve to increase her wealth and influence.

In a flash as brilliant as the first lighting of a bowl of luftall oil, Hranna saw herself managing not just her own village but others as well, running a vast network of trade up and down the coast. Again, she was not daunted that such a thing had never been accomplished, at least not in living memory. She was a legend now and would accomplish the sort of things that legendary heroes did, like uniting many villages under one leader. Suddenly, Inoah was simply one of many chiefs and no longer the be all and end all of her existence. Hranna began to sincerely hope that he might choose another bride so that she would be free to pursue her new-found ambitions. If he tried to take her, she might have to exercise her right to stab him, which would be a pity.

First, though, she had to survive and to reach Rolly's people alive.

They were making good time over the ice. Rolly was strong, despite his wound.

They were past their previous campsite and nearing the rock outcropping that she and her father had put against their backs while they weathered a bad winter storm. They could have died that night.

As if thinking of trouble could summon it, Hranna noticed Bin raise her head and flick her short, white tail. Nar's head shot up too, but his tail remained down. Hranna inhaled sharply.

Rolly must have felt her breath. "Do they always do that?"

Hranna shook her head. She realized that with her on his back, Rolly could not see her head movement. She vocalized her thoughts. "Only when danger is near."

"Haven't we had enough danger already?" Rolly chuckled at his own joke. The movement of his diaphragm hurt him and her as well.

Hranna knew that the ice never stopped setting dangerous traps, but she did not say as much to Rolly.

"It may be nothing," she said. "Look, Nar is not worried." She pointed over Rolly's shoulder to Nar's tail, which was flush against his fluffy bottom. Rolly's eyes followed her arm down her mittened finger. He watched the backside of the skisen as closely as Hranna. If Nar's tail went up, thought Hranna, it meant they were facing a serious threat, like a pack of wollen or, worse, a big browen.

Hranna whistled a comforting tune to her skisen. Bin lowered her tail. But for the rest of the day, Hranna watched the skisen carefully. The three of them had been together so long that she could read their body language as readily as that of any of her family or friends. Bin was anxious. Nar was trying to act nonchalant. Hranna admired his bravado. If there was danger out there, it was better not to let it know you were scared.

At midday, Hranna insisted that they mount the nearest snow drift before they took a rest. She didn't let the skisen browse for food. Hranna kept them close to the sled. It didn't require much effort, neither animal seemed inclined to wander. Occasionally, Bin raised her head and flicked her tail. Hranna kept a close watch on Nar. She could see nothing on the horizon; but, as so often happens, the nervousness of an animal affected its master. Hranna couldn't relax. She leaned against the sled for support. Her hand touched the bone handle of her knife, checking to make sure it could be removed quickly without getting caught on the sheath. It was as much preparation as she could make for an unknown threat that might not even exist.

The hunting pole had been retrieved from the dead luftall and replaced on the sled. The second foreshaft was stashed next to her tent. Maybe she should have Rolly carry it, just in case.

Hranna took the hafted foreshaft off the sled and handed it to Rolly.

"Trouble?"

"I don't know. Hang it around your waist."

For her midday meal, instead of luftall oil, Hranna drank water from her flagon and swallowed the contents of one of Rolly's metal pouches—twisting and untwisting the lid like a child with a new toy. The taste was sweet and foreign. Her people preferred salty flavors, but the change wasn't bad.

"That one is called chocolate," Rolly told her.

Hranna could easily get used to the strong, burnt taste. Perhaps if Rolly's people needed another luftall she could bargain for more chocolate. The idea appealed to her mightily.

The drinks were also refreshing. Rolly had explained that some contained medicine that allowed the drinker to work harder. He was drinking these. Others, like the one she drank, were useful for energy in the same way she ate luftall oil while on a hunt.

Rolly checked the drawings in his book.

"If we keep up this pace, we'll reach the place where we first met." He replaced the book into a large pocket on the front of his jacket. His hand must have brushed against the moondial. He pulled it out of his pocket and looked at it wistfully before replacing it. "We can stay there for the night. After that, it's only a few day's journey to my camp."

Hranna had been leaning on the sled. She whistled for the skisen and hopped around them, attaching the harnesses. Rolly joined her, helping with his good hand. They didn't speak. There was no need. Both knew what to do.

Rolly knelt in the snow, allowing Hranna to get on his back. Once secured, they set off again.

When they reached the site where they had first met, they stopped for the night.

Hranna insisted that they leave the sled on the other side of the snowdrift. If they were being tracked, perhaps the creature would take the luftall and leave them alone.

In the small valley on the other side of the snowdrift, Rolly checked his old hole.

"It's still good." He crawled out. "I could widen it for you."

Hranna snorted in derision. She might have subdued her pride enough to allow him to carry her, but she was not sleeping with him in a wollen hole.

Rolly took the hafted foreshaft off his belt and tested the weight of it in his hands. "It's safer if we stay together."

Only if it's not a pack of wollen after us, thought Hranna. Two people in that hole would just make their meal more convenient.

Interpreting her silence correctly, Rolly shrugged. "Whatever makes you happy."

He helped her set up the tent. His massive weight fixed the luftall poles in place deeply and quickly. As he arranged the top of the tent over the poles, she moved around the base, lashing the two halves together. The tent was assembled in short order. They made a good team, even with their injuries, or perhaps because of their injuries. They needed each other. Hranna felt her pride melt just a bit.

"You could join me in the tent."

Rolly looked at her and back at the patched animal skin. He raised his eyebrows, as if he doubted the soundness of the construction.

"It would be a little tight."

"Fine," Hranna said. "Forget it."

"I mean, thanks for the offer—"

"Forget it. Sleep in your hole." Her hand went automatically to the old injury on her ear.

"It's just, I think my feet would stick out."

Hranna crawled into the tent without looking back. She lashed the door flaps together tightly. She lay out flat, pulling a skisen fur blanket over her shoulders. Her boots hit the front of the tent. She calmed down a little. Rolly was much taller than she was, and she had built the tent to fit her and, of course, Bin. That old skisen probably wouldn't have liked being displaced by Rolly anyway. She felt a cool breeze as the front flap opened. She found herself hoping it was Rolly. Hranna was mildly annoyed when Bin crawled in beside her.

***

Hranna was awakened by a cry of pain. Bin jumped out of her sleepy embrace, putting her sharp horn through the top of the tent. Fine snow filtered through the new hole, dusting Hranna's cheek and helping wake her from a deep sleep.

The cry came again.

Bin bolted out of the tent, collapsing it around Hranna and dragging it, with her inside, halfway up the snow bank. The sudden movement jarred her leg, sending a jolt of pain that almost made her vomit.

Hranna struggled to get out of the tent. She had sewn it so tight together that she would have to locate the front flap to get out. At the next cry of pain, Hranna pulled her knife from the sheath and made a new exit in the tent. Rolly came up alongside her, the hafted foreshaft in his hand.

Although it was nighttime, because the sun never set, they could see as clearly as if it was morning.

There was no darkness to fear, only the danger that awaited them. Another cry came from the other side of the snow drift. This time Hranna recognized it.

"That was Nar."

"Where?"

Hranna struggled toward the top of the drift. Rolly put a hand under her arm, helping her along. Hranna scanned the horizon. She saw the sled. The luftall meat was scattered over the ice. She could not see Nar or Bin. She whistled for the skisen, but they didn't come. Bin's tracks raced away from the drift. With her injured leg, there was no way she could track them.

She feared for her skisen. But there were few things on the ice that could injure a healthy male skisen like Nar and fewer things that could get close enough to the fast animal to do damage.

"Stay here," Rolly said. "Yell if you see anything."

He walked cautiously toward the sled and began collecting the luftall meat. It seemed a foolish thing to do, especially if something big was after that meat, until Hranna considered that the survival of his crew depended on him bringing the meat back to camp. Just as he had risked his life to get the food, he would do so again to protect it.

Hranna sheathed her knife. She turned around and began hopping backwards down the snow drift, using her hands stretched out front to help keep her balance. Once at the bottom, she hopped over to Rolly and put one hand on the sled. She pulled out her knife. Hranna could see nothing on the ice, but she wasn't taking any chances. Whatever had scattered the luftall meat might still be nearby. She called to her skisen again. Even if she and Rolly saved the meat, if they had no skisen to pull it, his people would be out of luck.

"There." Hranna pointed. Rolly looked up.

In the distance, Hranna saw the two skisen returning. She whistled. They did not speed to her side. Something was wrong. Nar was not moving well.

As the pair neared the sled, Hranna saw that Nar was lame in one leg and was leaving a bright, red trail of blood behind him. Hranna wanted to rush to her injured friend. Rolly held her back. She shook off his big, gloved hand.

"Let them come to us."

She knew he was right. They should stick together. But the wait was intolerable.

Finally, the skisen reached the sled. Bin nuzzled Hranna's hand. She hopped around Nar's side. The tip of his curved horn was covered with blood. Deep gashes ran down his side, matting his soft white fur together. He was unable to put weight on his back foot. Hranna nearly cried. She doubted whether he could recover from such an injury. If one of his bones was broken, he would have to be put down.

"What could have done this?" said Rolly.

Rolly, of course, didn't know. But to Hranna, the answer was obvious. There was only one thing that could have made those marks. "A browen," Hranna whispered.

"A what?"

"Browen," she repeated. "Big and covered in coarse white fur with a dark patch on its chest." She didn't add that no one saw the browen's chest and lived. A brace of brave men might kill a browen. To have its fur line one's hut was a great honor. It was something that two invalids like them had no hope of obtaining.

"Think it's still out there?"

"Nar must have interrupted its feast." Hranna patted the wounded skisen on its head. The browen must have been tracking them since the cliff, waiting for an opportunity to strike. They had been lucky that the browen had pillaged the sled at night instead of attacking them on the ice. It must not have known how weak they were. Rolly's plan of sleeping in a hole in the snow bank was beginning to sound like a good idea.

Nar had protected them and had saved the supplies and the lives of Rolly's people, but at a terrible price.

"We need to get moving," Rolly said. He took the magic white powder out of his bag and dusted Nar's injured flank.

"We cannot outrun a browen." Hranna stated it simply. The browen would do what it wanted to do. Once again, Hranna had no control over her own fate.

"We haven't even seen it yet. How do we know it's still out there?"

"Once you see it, it's too late," said Hranna.

"We can leave something for it," Rolly said.

Hranna shook her head in exasperation at his foolishness. He seemed still ignorant of their danger. "You said no luftall can be spared." They had discussed it so many times already. It was the reason that Hranna had been riding on Rolly's back.

"I didn't mean luftall." Rolly patted Nar's head. The skisen gave a low moan of pain.

When she realized what he meant, Hranna recoiled from the thought.

"It was just an idea," he said.

Hranna considered it again. Though she loved the skisen, she would sacrifice it if she must. Nar could hardly survive the injury even with Rolly's magic powder.

"Even if it feeds on Nar, it will continue to hunt us." She had to make Rolly understand their plight. The browens were fiercely territorial. "It will kill us one by one."

"If we reached my people, I think we'd be safe."

"That is two more days?"

"At least." Rolly nodded.

"My village is closer."

"I thought you wouldn't take me there."

Hranna didn't respond. She hadn't intended to take Rolly to her village. She needed the wealth that he carried in order to ensure her own survival. The villagers would insist on a share of his metal, even though it was Hranna who had risked her life hunting the luftall on the ice. Of course, she wouldn't have had to do that, and wouldn't be missing a foot if she had shared with the village in the first place.

Now, with a browen stalking them, she had little choice. If they made it to the village, she would live, for now. Her people probably would not kill Rolly on sight. She could make up a good story about how he saved her life during a hunt.

Hranna made up her mind. She turned the knife in her hand and reached lovingly toward Nar's neck as if to stroke the poor creature's fur. If her old friend had to die, it would be by Hranna's own hand.

Rolly grabbed her elbow.

"Not yet," he said.

"Why not?"

"I still have this." Rolly pulled out the cylindrical red tube—the one out of which the star had flown, burning the mother luftall.

"Will it kill the browen?"

Rolly shook his head in the negative. "No, but it should scare it off. I have one shot left." He tucked the cylinder into his belt. "If it follows us, we try to scare it off. If we can't scare it off, we sacrifice Nar, but not before we're sure that we have to."

"It will ambush us on the ice if we move forward."

"Maybe so." Rolly set his hands on his hips and waited for Hranna's response.

His plan sounded totally unreasonable. Yet she did not want to kill Nar and saw little hope of survival either way. Probably Rolly was correct. The longer they waited to kill Nar, the more time it would give them to reach safety.

Apparently Rolly had tired of waiting on her decision. He motioned for Hranna to get on his back.

Grudgingly she assented. Hranna hopped over to him with her arms crossed, "What will you do if the browen attacks?"

"Drop you and run." Though his back was already to her, Hranna could tell he was smiling, trying to make light of the situation.

She hopped onto his back and squeezed close to him while he connected and tightened her harness.

His next move surprised her. He hitched Bin to the sled, then picked up the end of Nar's line in his good hand. He looped it around his shoulder.

"Are you going to pull me and the sled?" Hranna asked.

"Is there any other way?"

Hranna had to admit that she could think of nothing else. The grief at the injury to Nar had clouded her ability to reason. She should have realized that Nar could not pull the sled. And, of course, Bin could not haul it on her own. Rolly must have recognized all this at once. He also must have known that she never would have gotten on his back if he told her his stupidly chivalrous plan.

They went slowly at first. Rolly's footprints dug deep into the snow. He bent over nearly parallel to the ground. From her perch on his back, Hranna thought she could reach out and touch the ice. As the sled started moving, the load became easier. Rolly straightened up a bit.

Despite the discomfort radiating from her missing foot, riding on Rolly's back over the ice was pleasant but not carefree. Nar's occasional mewls of pain troubled her. She hated that her long-time companion was suffering while she could do nothing to help. The walk was also clouded by the almost certain death hunting them in the shape of a browen's fangs and claws. Hranna touched her disfigured ear. It was the least of her worries now. Hranna gave into her earlier impulse. She put her face into the back of Rolly's hood and breathed deeply the smell of cut trees.

Chapter 5

Their ragged band trudged wordlessly across the ice, resting as little as possible and even then only on top of a tall snowdrift where they could see the ice around them. Hranna watched Bin's tail, looking for any sign that the browen was coming for them. Rolly checked the wind using the small metal flag mounted on his moondial.

"The wind is blowing in our direction."

Hranna said nothing.

"It means that the browen can't hunt us from behind. Which means we will make better time than it does."

To her, it meant that the browen would likely circle around them, springing a deadly trap farther down their path. It would almost be a source of comfort to know that the beast was behind them. That would at least put a sense of urgency into each weary step.

Rolly took a drink from one of his metal pouches. He dropped it to the ground. Hranna retrieved it, placing the precious, whisper-thin metal into an inner pocket.

"That was my last one," he said. One look at Rolly and Hranna could see that, like a luftall pierced through the ice and fighting against the hunter's sled, Rolly was reaching the end of his rope.

They started down the snowdrift, moving one step closer toward safety and home.

"So I get to see the place where you grew up?"

Hranna was surprised Rolly could speak through all the effort it took to carry her and pull the sled.

"What there is of it."

Hranna suspected that Rolly, with his magical tools and seemingly unlimited supply of metal, would not be impressed with their small village by the sea. She also suspected that he might not like the welcome he received. Hranna hoped that her father was well enough to receive the visitor. She knew she could talk to her father: make him understand how much a good relationship with Rolly and his people could mean the village. Future trade with Rolly's people would be invaluable. There was also the knowledge they possessed of how to record their words and how to bottle the stars in the heavens. If her people could learn such skills, they would prosper.

Hranna looked around as familiar landmarks began to crop up. To one like Rolly, each white hill might look the same, but to Hranna, they were as familiar as the lines on her father's face. She noted that they were actually making decent time. At this pace, they might reach her village in the morning of the next day, provided Rolly could hold out that long. If he could not, if he needed to sleep, she did not know how to construct the burrow in the ice. Also, he had lost his digging tool while battling the luftall back at the cliffs. Her tent was too small for two, not to mention the big hole Bin had put in it, rushing out of it earlier that morning when the browen first struck and dragging Hranna with it up the hill. She had had to slice her way out of it.

Suddenly, Bin's head went up, followed quickly by her tail. Nar, who had been hobbling behind them, let out a fierce bellow.

Rolly charged ahead drawing the sled with little help from Bin to the top of the nearest drift. He untied himself from the sled and from Hranna as well. Her foot hit the ground. She steadied herself on the sled. Rolly unhitched Bin. He pulled out his red tube and scanned the horizon.

Hranna looked not at the landscape but at her skisen. They would tell her more than her eyes could about the browen's location. Nar finally joined them at the top of the snow drift. His curved horn, which had been drooping most of the day, now stood upright at its full height. Bin's eyes were wide. She was looking off to the right. Hranna bent at the waist pushing her injured leg out behind her for balance. She picked up a handful of snow and tossed it into the air, repeating Rolly's trick from the cliff. The snow drifted to her left.

"Rolly."

"I see it."

"The wind changed directions."

Rolly and Hranna turned in unison, just in time to see the browen erupt from the snow at the base of the drift. The creature rose upon its short hind legs, baring its front claws and the black patch on its chest. The browen's roar rattled over the barren, white landscape.

Hranna pulled her knife. Rolly, seeing its glint, shoved Hranna. Her one leg could not compensate. She fell backwards down the drift—away from the browen. Bin, showing uncommon good sense, ran with Hranna and stood next to her prone form. Bin was the only one in the group who could outrun the beast. Hranna was tempted to try to ride the skisen as she had when she was a child. But she could not leave Rolly, not after he had saved her from the luftall.

Hranna clambered on her hands and knees up the drift. She managed to keep hold of her knife.

She could see Rolly clearly now. He had the red tube lowered in his good hand, pressed away from his chest. He fired as the browen crested the ridge. A brilliant red star burst from his hands. It flew toward the browen, catching the beast in the side of its head. The star bounced off the top of the beast's thick brow and shot into the starless sky.

The browen didn't stop. It didn't even pause in its lumbering gait toward Rolly. Hranna would not reach him in time.

Rolly pulled something out of his coat. It was as long as Hranna's forearm and pointed at the end. It looked like a luftall's hind tusk. She remembered what he had said about taking something from the beast that had injured them both. She almost smiled. He had taken the tusk that had gored him and was using it against the browen, having apparently forgotten about the hafted skisen horn hanging from his side.

Rolly yelled. He threw open his arms, even his injured one, and made himself look big. He charged the browen. Hranna couldn't believe his bravery or his stupidity. Maybe in his sleep-deprived state it seemed like a good idea.

The browen swatted him aside with the back of its paw. Had it used the front, clawed side, Rolly would have been finished. As it was, he flew through the air, landing in a crumpled pile.

The browen seemed intent on the sled, laden as it was with luftall meat. Well, if that's what it wanted, Hranna didn't see a way to stop it, though it meant Rolly's people might starve. She found herself wondering whether the browen would ignore her and Rolly, letting them escape while it concentrated on the sled. Hranna thought it unlikely given how territorial the beasts were.

Hranna lowered herself in the snow hoping to stay out of the browen's line of sight. She scuttled around the lip of the snow drift toward the place where Rolly had fallen and now lay limp.

The browen slowed as it approached the sled. Its nose panned the air. Hranna wondered why it had paused. Then Nar stepped around the sled. His normally gray horn was brown with dried blood. There was a corresponding wound on the browen's shoulder. Apparently these two had some unfinished business.

The browen began to slowly circle around Nar, looking for a way to get past the wicked horn.

Hranna knelt beside Rolly. His breathing was shallow. He was as stiff as a log. And one of his legs was twitching. Hranna shook him. He came awake with a start and lunged at her with the luftall horn. Its sharp point pierced her jacket, going straight through her bicep.

Hranna sat back with a grunt.

Rolly's eyes cleared. He saw what he'd done.

"Hranna—"

"Pull it out."

She didn't blame him. He had been knocked out and had woken up fighting. She had seen it happen before, during a drunken brawl in the village.

"Hranna, I'm so sorry."

He was focused on the tusk sticking out of her arm. He could not see the fight that Hranna was witnessing over his shoulder.

The browen was leaking blood from several nicks on its face and shoulders. It left giant red prints in the snow from where the blood ran down its front limbs and also from the blood on its claws where it had scored another hit on Nar's haunch. Nar's wound had been reopened by a fresh gash. He was wielding his horn like a knife, flicking it back and forth, but Hranna could tell that her old friend was tiring.

The browen lunged. Nar was too slow on the counter-stroke. The browen's teeth sank into Nar's front shoulder, The weight of the heavy beast bore Nar to the ice, pinning him there for the death stroke.

"No," Hranna screamed. She pulled the tusk out of her arm and threw it in one motion. Blood gushed from her now open wound. The tusk traveled in a lazy arc, landing ineffectually against the browen's head.

It turned toward the new annoyance. Taking its bloody paw off of Nar, the browen walked slowly toward Hranna and Rolly, who had not yet fully recovered his senses.

The beast was so close that she could clearly see each gnarled tooth in its fearsome mouth. Its breath smoked from the battle it had done with Nar. Hranna drew her knife. She waited calmly for death.

Hranna caught movement out of the corner of her eye. Bin was bearing down on the browen. The beast was preoccupied. Bin hit the browen in the side with her straight horn.

The impact knocked the browen back a few steps. It roared with pain.

Bin removed her horn and made ready to stab him again. She was rewarded with a claw to the face.

Bin fell back, bleeding.

Hranna stood as best she could and raised the knife her father had given her.

The browen stood too and showed her its chest. The great white beast was beautiful in its power. Behind its back a group of high clouds chased across the sun. Hranna appreciated all that she had been given.

The browen stumbled forward. It wasn't the kind of attack she had been expecting. Embedded in its back was a curved skisen horn with the skisen still attached.

Nar had reentered the fray.

His horn stuck deep into the browen's lower back. It must have hooked onto a rib, because the browen could not shake Nar off of his back. The pair rolled down the snow drift locked together.

As they reached the bottom, Hranna heard a sickening crack. Nar lay limp, his neck broken under the browen's weight. Still the browen could not dislodge the dead, brave skisen. It tried to crawl back up toward Hranna. It collapsed. The browen rose again only to collapse again. There it lay, its breath coming in raspy wheezes. Hranna rejected the urge to end the creature's suffering. It was still too dangerous. And she had an injured skisen and an insensible man to deal with, not to mention a gaping hole in her arm. She would let the animal die naturally; then she would take its coat and Nar's too, to remember him by on cold nights.

Chapter 6

The party that traveled from her village to investigate the shooting star saw a very strange sight.

"Three legs sticking out of your tent—" A wet cough interrupted her father's admonishment.

"I know, Papa." Hranna was sitting on a rough-hewn bench in the tent of meeting. Her elbows were on her knees. Her head hung below her shoulders. The warmth of the nearby fire, smokelessly fueled by a compress of wood chips soaked in luftall oil, barely reached her. She had been in the village an hour but had not yet shed her outer furs. Even if she had, the tradition of sharing a fire with her father after the hunt brought little comfort. She was concerned about Rolly and about her father's nagging cough.

"Four legs would have been a scandal," her father paused to breathe. "Three legs will be talked about for years!"

"I know, Papa."

The small village was already talking about them: about the stranger adorned with metal like a tree's first frost and about the girl with one foot.

The villagers who had come to investigate the mystery of the red star stumbled upon Hranna and Rolly asleep together in her small tent. She had ransacked his backpack, using what was left of the white powder and the spiderwebbing on her punctured arm and on Bin's face. She assembled the tent around Rolly where he had fallen, doing her best with one good arm to patch the holes where Bin's horn and her knife had punched through its roof earlier.

She cleaned the two dead animals enough that their meat would not spoil. Afterward, she crawled in beside Rolly who was already fast asleep.

Bin, who was used to sleeping next to Hranna, voiced her annoyance in a series of loud brays. Hranna slept right through the noise.

It took the villagers some effort to wake her. No amount of effort on her part or theirs could wake Rolly.

They helped her finish skinning the animals, taking as much of the browen and skisen meat as they could manage. They would have to make a return trip to retrieve the rest, provided a pack of wollen didn't find it first. Hranna also took as prizes the teeth and claws of the browen as well as its pelt. She also took Nar's horn and his soft fur coat.

Hranna could tell what the villagers were thinking from the way they looked at her askance and from what they said and what they omitted. You did not live among a people for as long as she had without being able to read each other. She looked like them, covered in tanned animal skins wrapped with sinew, hood thrown over braided black hair, skin that was so brown next to Rolly's. They might look the same, but they did not think the same. She could tell that they were afraid of the stranger and of her by association.

Hranna nearly cried when they skinned Nar, but tears would only burn her skin. She was tough. Hranna was a woman of the wastes and a hunter of the ice. Yet the work wore her down. She accepted a ride on a neighbor's sled, but not before stashing Rolly's backpack inside her rolled up tent. She didn't know what the villagers' reaction would have been to the bag and all its dangling riches that rightfully belonged to her in reward for the successful hunt and in compensation for the loss of her foot.

The villagers were impressed enough with the small pieces of metal that hung from his jacket. Hranna knew the small tabs were used to open pockets, but the villagers had assumed they were some kind of decoration. She didn't disabuse them of their conclusions. After all, the moondial and the precious book were in one of those pockets where she hoped they would remain undisturbed.

Rolly never regained consciousness as they loaded him onto a sled. Hranna could not tell if it was the effect of the blow from the browen or a reaction to the medicine he had taken to stay awake and alert for so long. They took him directly to the healer's hut.

Yansil the healer, having finished with Rolly, was now kneeling in front of Hranna in the tent of meeting, examining her wounds. The old woman smelled as though she'd slept in the skisen pens. The stench was an aftereffect of the medicine she brewed which, though it benefited the village greatly, did not make Yansil a welcome guest. Some claimed she could work magic with her brews. Hranna wasn't convinced.

Hranna looked around the large room as the healer probed at her bicep. The fresh injury was still sore, and she did not want the healer or her father to see just how much the probing fingers stung.

The tent of meeting was a low, circular room supported at the perimeter by a series of tree-trunks dug into the frozen ground under the ice. Hranna doubted it would even be possible to dig deep enough to find solid ground out on the wastes. The snow just went on forever, in every direction but up—except in a snowstorm, she thought, when the snow above was as thick as the snow below.

Floor to ceiling, the tent was lined with the best furs from centuries of hunts. Several short benches (the brush trees near the village grew no taller than Hranna, though considerably thicker) were arranged at the center of the tent near the fire. These were usually reserved for persons of authority. He father sat on the tallest stool now, just as he did in all of her memories.

Yansil poked at the stump of Hranna's leg. Hranna flinched automatically but felt no pain. The healer disconnected Rolly's tourniquet from Hranna's upper calf. She did not bleed. Rolly's powder and the webbing must indeed hold some magic power.

The old woman was fascinated with the spiderwebbing on Hranna's leg and on her shoulder, yet Yansil managed to remain her dour old self. Her personality was nearly as sour as her smell.

"You should be dead."

Yansil closely inspected Rolly's belt and its metal buckle. Hranna could tell the woman was wondering whether she might lay claim to the item as a medical tool.

"It is his belt," said Hranna. "Will you keep it for him? When he recovers, I'm sure he will thank you graciously for your care."

With hardly a thought, Hranna had gracefully executed the sort of subtle political move for which her father was so well regarded. The healer gained some gratitude toward Hranna, who had done virtually nothing, and a corresponding goodwill extended toward Rolly who might bestow wealth on the healer for her services.

It wouldn't do to have the healer wishing he was dead, ready like all the rest to pluck his corpse like a luftall.

"Of course," the woman nodded grimly. "He is still unconscious. I can do nothing for him."

"He told me that he must sleep in order to recover from the magic he used to fight the browen." Hranna had lied about Rolly. They thought he was a sorcerer. Hranna thought he had a better chance of waking up with his metal and with his clothes if her people thought he had the power to pull stars out of a moonless sky like the one they had seen and come to investigate.

Hranna reached a hand into her pocket, running it over the smooth sides of the medicine pouch Rolly had dropped so nonchalantly to the ice. Was it so different than magic?

Her father's tone was accusing, "You were in the tent alone, with a stranger."

"I told you, Papa, he saved my life. He was injured." She wanted to add that nothing had happened, but such information was too personal to discuss in front of the healer.

"Inoah came to see me," said her father.

Hranna sighed. "When?"

"Just before you entered."

Hranna had been in the tent of meeting for only a short time, having first seen to Bin and to the contents of her sled. She had delivered the luftall meat to Strau, the unnaturally thin keeper of the village stores, telling him that the luftall belonged to the stranger. After all, he had killed it.

Hranna looked from her father to the healer. There were things that the village should not hear and probably would if the old woman stuck around.

"Yansil, I'm sure that you have done everything you can for me."

"But—" the old healer objected.

"Thank you, Yansil." Hranna took the old woman's hand and helped her to her feet, a sure sign of her intent to speak to her father alone. "I will visit you and the stranger as soon as I am able."

The healer collected her tools, including Rolly's belt. She handed Hranna a tall piece of wood with a notch at one end. "For balance."

Hranna nodded. She'd seen a crutch before. Hers was not the first leg to go lame.

Yansil, bent as she was by old age, hobbled out of the tent.

Hranna returned her attention to the matter at hand. It didn't surprise her that Inoah had visited her father.

The chief continued, "He says we should kill the stranger."

Hranna struggled to maintain her composure. Her father might be testing her, trying to provoke her into revealing some feelings for Rolly. "Papa, you cannot kill him. He is a wizard, and his people are rich."

"You told me of their village of metal, though I hardly believe such a fairy tale. But is Inoah wrong?"

Hranna raised her head. She looked keenly into her father's face, sensing his thoughts. She held her breath.

"Do you know why our villages are so far apart?" he asked Hranna.

She wanted to say that it was because they did not have writing or the sophisticated tools that Rolly's people had.

"Because there is not enough." Her father stoked the fire. A single spark drifted toward the low ceiling. "The ice can only provide for so many."

Hranna started to argue, but her father raised his hand, urging her to let him finish.

"Can the wastes support our people and his? If they come, how many will come? And if they come in force can they kill us, take our land?"

"You sound like Inoah."

"Inoah sounds like a chief," said her father. The implication stung. Had she been born male, Hranna would have been chief.

As it was, the distinction was going to fall to Inoah, a cousin (weren't they all?) and a distinguished hunter. Hranna might once have wanted to be his wife, but meeting Rolly and seeing a vision of another kind of future had changed all that. Besides, she wasn't sure whether Inoah, or anyone else for that matter, wanted a one-legged wife who had spent a night on the ice with a stranger. Unless she was a rich, one-legged wife, in which case, some exception might be arranged.

"Papa, his people had only seven or eight days of food. That was five days ago at least."

"The luftall you brought belongs to the village."

"He killed it."

Her father coughed into his hand. "My people carried it off the ice."

Hranna felt blood rushing to her face. Where the meager fire had failed to warm her, this argument heated her cheeks. "What of the browen?"

Her father looked at her with unabashed pride reflecting light the fire in his eyes. "In all my years, I never killed a browen." He stirred the fire with the thin rib of a luftall. "The kill does not belong to your man. It belongs to you and to your skisen. Its meat and its coat and every piece of the browen, and of your Nar, belongs to you. These are the rules of the hunt as you well know."

Rolly was not "her man." Hranna fumed.

Her father continued, "Besides, all the meat under the ice can do no good for his people, since we do not know where they are."

Hranna thought she might be able to find them, using Rolly's book.

"If he wakes," said her father, "we will see what he is willing to pay for meat."

There it was. Hranna's fears and suspicions were confirmed. Her father would bargain directly with Rolly, cutting her out of the profit that she had negotiated and almost died for. It would not matter to Rolly whether he traded with her or with her father.

Even if he wished to honor their agreement, Hranna had nothing to trade with and no control over the distribution of the village's meat supplies. Browen meat might satisfy hunger, but its fat would not burn.

Hranna no longer had the power to fulfill her side of the bargain. She certainly could not go back out on the ice to hunt.

Whatever metal her father received from Rolly in trade would be distributed equally among the village, per their customs. Yet, her father, as the village chief, had a knack for ending up with the choicest items in trade, which he often distributed among his close friends or to those whose goodwill he needed. Hranna could almost hear him calculating the number of metal tabs on Rolly's blue clothing.

Hranna expelled her breath audibly. It was time to come clean with her father about the hunt. Perhaps he would help her once he understood her motives.

"I had a deal with him already. If I delivered a luftall to his people, I would receive a good weight of metal."

Her father narrowed his eyes, examining her carefully.

She had no choice but to continue. "If I had the metal, I thought I might marry Inoah or—"

"You are the chief's daughter. You may marry whomever you choose." Her father coughed again, ending with a raspy wheeze.

"Yet no one has asked me—"

"Probably afraid you'd spurn them with the edge of your knife," he said with a twinkle in his eye. "Besides, I will find you the right man. Have I not all the wealth you need? Why shouldn't Inoah be yours if you choose?"

Hranna let her head fall back down below her shoulders. Her father did not understand. He could not conceive of his not being chief. He could not accept his mortality. He did not or could not realize that everything he had as chief would belong to Inoah. He had nothing with which to tempt that man into marriage. Already it was too late. She suspected that, even if her father were well enough to make a match, every man in the village would politely decline. There were only so many eligible men in her village. And only a madman would marry her in the shadow of Inoah's reign as village chief.

Hranna forced herself to smile. "As you say, Father." She knew that arguing would do no good, nor did she have the desire to waste their precious time together.

Her father reached over and patted Hranna on the knee. "Tell me again how you hunted the luftall on top of the ice."

Hranna was happy to tell him, and if he fell asleep in the middle of the story, as so often he did these days, she would wait patiently until he awoke and continue as though she had never stopped.

But in those quiet moments, while her father snored lightly by the fire, his lungs sometimes catching and grasping for breath, Hranna considered her fate.

Rolly, though he was injured and unconscious at present, might ultimately survive. Hranna was not sure that the same could be said for her. At best, she might share Yansil the Healer's fate, growing old, alone, covered in wrinkles from head to foot. Or she might be banished to the ice when her father died, which would mean a slow death like the one Rolly's people might be suffering even as she and her father spoke.

The flame on the fire moved suddenly toward Hranna. Someone had entered the tent. The flame arched its back, longing to go where it could breathe freely. Hranna turned to see who had entered. Inoah's huge frame filled the doorway. In the firelight she could barely see his face beneath the drawn hood. Inoah did not look happy.

Chapter 7

Inoah strode over to where Hranna and her father sat, keeping warm by the fire. Like Hranna, he was still wearing his outer skins. He too had just returned from a hunt, though not as long nor as successful. Even the most gifted hunters were not always rewarded.

Lurking behind Inoah was the village waterwan, the man who spoke to the spirits of the ocean. Yanka was every bit as small and shriveled as Inoah was huge. The spiritist looked as though the freezing salt water in which he bathed to see his visions had permanently withered his skin like a piece of dried luftall. Hranna had never liked him. He had predicted her mother's death a week before she took ill. That he had been right only made her hate him more.

Yanka's sharp nose poked the air. He grimaced, muttering under his breath to no one in particular, "Smells like skisen excrement in here." Inoah ignored him as did Hranna. The waterwan must have been referring to Yansil's earlier presence. Yanka had always disliked the healer for some reason.

"Inoah." Hranna did not rise to greet him. As the chief's daughter she still outranked him socially, even if it was in name only. The rest of the villagers were already falling in line.

Inoah took the bench across from her. Even seated, he towered over her the same way Rolly did, only, with Inoah, there was also plenty of mass to his bulk. The wooden bench accepted his weight with a bent resignation. He pulled his hood back to reveal a long braid of fine black hair, just like hers. His curved nose shone in relief against the firelight. Hranna had to admit that Inoah was handsome; a hunter; a leader of men; and, if she wanted to survive, her future husband. At times like these, she almost forgot why she didn't want to marry him.

Till he opened his mouth.

"I see you were too sour to eat." Inoah studied her missing foot.

There it was, his infuriating attitude.

"I was too good to eat all at once." Hranna responded.

"Ha!" Her father had awoken with Inoah's entrance. "You two already sound like an old married couple."

Hranna winced. It was a sensitive subject. She wished her father would be more circumspect. His skills of subtle manipulation had atrophied along with his frail body.

"Hranna married and tending a man's fire?" said Inoah, sounding bemused.

If the fur on Hranna's neck had been real, it would have risen to the challenge. "Remind us what you got on your hunt?"

"The baby luftall you took is hardly—"

"I took it on the open ice."

"As you say."

"And I killed a browen." Hranna's eyes flashed with triumph. Was not the fur of the browen being prepared for her rooms?

"The way I heard the story, your skisen killed the browen."

Hranna began to protest, but Inoah warded her off with a shake of his hand, indicating that this wasn't a fight that he wanted to have. "Nar was a good skisen. Remember when I sold him to you? I knew he'd take care of you, and he did."

Hranna hadn't thought Inoah even remembered the transaction. They had been so young.

Hranna checked her emotions. If Inoah was bringing up the past, it wasn't to reminisce. Either he meant something by the remark or wanted to lower her defenses to what came next. He was trying to win her over and not doing a half-bad job of it.

"Nar was brave," said Hranna. "I've taken the horn that killed the browen. I will hunt with it to remember him."

Inoah stared into the fire.

"Are your hunting days not at an end?" Yanka, the village waterwan took up the idea that was surely circulating in Inoah's mind.

Hranna suspected a ploy. Inoah would let Yanka deliver the bad news. Her father had done the same thing, remaining likeable and above the fray while his henchmen handled the dirty work. Though Hranna understood the tactic, it was hard to respect a man who didn't clean his own kills.

For Hranna, who had sat with her father in the tent of meeting since she was a young girl, this conversation was to her what a dance around the fire of the gathering was to any simple village girl. It would take Inoah and Yanka years to perfect their routine. Meanwhile, Hranna could lead the conversation at will.

She sighed and added quite calmly, "If that is a prediction, Yanka, you may be right." She shrugged her shoulders in the demure way that came so easily to the other girls of the village. "What with my injury, it may be time to settle down."

"Hmm," Yanka nodded gravely. She knew that he was just buying time. He had expected her to lock horns like male skisen. They did not realize why the female skisen had a straight horn. When they struck, it was direct and to the heart. They did not play at head butting like the obtuse males.

"It is a shame that you did not retire sooner," said Yanka. "Your last hunt will be sung at the gatherings. But it may be difficult to find a man who would live in its shadow," he paused for emphasis, "or with your hindrances."

He was not only referring to her mangled leg. Hranna was shocked that they had arrived at the heart of the matter so quickly. For the first time, she began to doubt Inoah's fitness to rule the village, especially if he couldn't handle a simple negotiation like this.

And it was a negotiation.

Yanka's response was equally shocking. After months of speculation, the answer to her most basic question of survival had been delivered with no more anticipation than Rolly's blow to her arm. Yanka was telling her that Inoah would not marry her.

No, she decided, he was saying much more than that. He was saying that no man in the village would marry her.

Yanka had laid out Inoah's conditions for her continued stay in the village. Inoah had prefaced the remarks with his reference to their shared childhood, meaning that he would honor their past. But Yanka had delivered the point of the horn. If she remained in the village, she would never lead a normal life as a wife with a family.

There would be no one to give her father's knife to.

Hranna put her hand to the old scar at her ear. Inoah had not yet removed his eyes from the fire. Her father had drifted off to sleep again, the nuances of the conversation eluding his tired mind.

Hranna tried another approach. "I might have other qualities. Hidden traits that might commend me to some man, even a good man." It was the nearest she dared come to mentioning the treasure trove of metal that was on Rolly's backpack, hidden in her room.

Yanka began to reply. Inoah waved him off. His gesture was silent but powerful. He indicated with a tip of his head that Yanka should make a quiet exit so as not to disturb the old chief who had drowsed off.

As Yanka retreated into the cold, Inoah turned to face Hranna full on for the first time that evening. He was no longer talking at her sideways. He was giving her his full attention. Though she had known him as an awkward boy, the effect of his adult presence was impossible to dismiss.

"Yanka handled that pretty poorly, didn't he?" Inoah smiled conspiratorially. He was trying to draw her in. Hranna found her resistance to his charms had almost melted. Yet, was there any point in remaining obstinate when his intent had already been made so clear?

"Hranna, I am not an idiot. You know this." He let the remark sink in before continuing. "I've seen the metal on your friend. I know he could not have crossed the snow with only his clothing. He must have had some equipment. I accept that you buried it somewhere before my people arrived."

Hranna now understood the furtive looks that the villagers had given her when they arrived at her campsite earlier in the day. They had not been sent by her father but by Inoah. What's more, he did not suspect that the backpack was in her rooms. Or he did not have the gall to search her father's tent.

"Do you know where he came from?"

Hranna shook her head, no. At least she didn't have to lie.

"Hranna, even if you did return with a sled filled with metal, what did you think you would accomplish? What would stop someone from taking it from you?"

She looked instinctively at her father.

Inoah reached out and put a firm hand on Hranna's forearm. His grip was not tight, nor was it comforting. He was not trying to be her friend, but neither was he actively harming her. For all the politics she had observed with her father, none had prepared her to deal with a man who was simply telling her how it was.

"I am not going to marry you. Once, when we were young, I thought—" His eyes drifted over her shoulder momentarily. "I do not think you would be happy as my wife. As they say, 'Two hunters starve for want of a cook.'" Inoah cast a look of disdain in her father's direction as though he blamed her father for something, perhaps for the way she was raised. His look of disappointment echoed feelings she had had often enough. Still, it rankled to see such condemnation come from outside the family. Worse that it might be deserved. Perhaps if her mother had lived, things might have been different.

"I cannot allow you to marry another. You understand." His eyes squinted at this last statement. It was clear that Inoah felt uncomfortable discussing the subject. Hranna, who had grown up around skisen, needed no lessons. He would not allow her to be in a position where she might have an heir.

She nodded. Of course she understood his point. He was speaking her very thoughts. The only surprise was that Inoah was being so brutally honest. He obviously did not intend to let her show up in the village with a sled full of metal. Nor would he stand idly by while she bore children. He would brook no challenge to his rule. Hranna's practical side admired the efficiency of the conversation and the force of his will.

Inoah continued. "Bring me the blue man's treasure."

Though she was fully clothed and still in her outer furs, a chill ran down Hranna's spine. She did not need Yanka's skills of prognostication to know it was Inoah's final offer.

She had thought Inoah intended to spare her. And perhaps he did—but only for a price.

She ran the possibilities through her mind as though she were fishing a luftall, trying to predict where it would break through the ice. She could bring him the backpack now. Inoah would probably not kill her while her father remained chief. Rolly, on the other hand, would not be so lucky. If Inoah suddenly became wealthy, he would not have to trade.

However, even if she acknowledged the backpack, there was no guarantee that Inoah would spare her. As a boy he had been decent. Hranna knew better than most that decency was a nicety a chief could not afford.

Were there other options? When in danger or facing a problem during a hunt, Hranna's mind proved flexible. She bent her limited imagination to her will now. She saw a possibility. It was dangerous, but considering the alternatives...

"I hunted the luftall in exchange for his metal," she said. "I earned it with my leg as payment."

Inoah shrugged off her claim to the luftall and to the proceeds in the same way that her father had. It occurred to Hranna that Inoah might even have supplied her father with the finders-keepers argument during their earlier meeting. Still, Hranna knew that if she acceded too readily, Inoah might suspect her of harboring ulterior motives, which she certainly was forming as quickly as she could.

While this conversation had been unfortunate, it had nevertheless been enlightening. Hranna had been naive. She thought that if she survived the hunt and returned with a horde of metal, she might entice Inoah to marry her or might subvert his rule with her wealth.

Had she returned with the wealth, her life would have been forfeit. Her father had grown too weak to protect her. Even if she had the good sense to hide the wealth, the appearance of any piece of new metal would have caused a stir in the village; its source would soon have been discovered and the end result the same. In a way, this talk had saved her life.

She was strangely grateful to Inoah. He had shown Hranna another piece of the puzzle as to how life on the ice really worked. To someone who loved understanding systems and connections, this knowledge was a bit like a gift. She saw that, without the power to protect it, the possession of wealth was illusory.

As the chief's daughter, it was a lesson she'd never had to learn. As the unmarried and unprotected orphan of a soon-to-be-dead chief, she took the lesson to heart.

"As you say, Inoah. I too had hoped that you and I might—" She hung a look of defeat and of a crushed heart on her face. Inoah might not truly believe that she felt his rejection so deeply, but the male ego could be a powerful deceiver and a good distraction.

"I will retrieve the blue man's supplies," she took a deep breath, considering what came next, "in exchange for the life of the blue man." She did not ask for her own life. He had not directly threatened her. It would be a sign of weakness and perhaps even an insult to acknowledge so directly the implicit threat. He would understand the implications—that the deal she offered included herself as well, if she survived.

Inoah seemed relieved. Maybe he truly thought the ice would kill her, solving all his problems. "Agreed. You can take a skisen from my stable to replace Nar."

"No. I have the browen's teeth. I can trade them for what I need."

Inoah nodded. He understood. Neither of them would go onto the ice with a skisen that belonged to another, one she could not turn entirely to her will.

"What of your leg?" Inoah examined her with the same concern he might show for an injured skisen, which was actually quite a lot given his admiration for the creatures. Still, it was clear that she was nothing more than a tool to him, no more than any other villager under his charge and perhaps less.

"Do I have a choice?"

Inoah smiled genuinely for the first time. She remembered that smirk from his younger, carefree face. "I suppose not. Not if you care for the blue man."

"I cared for the metal he carried. I thought I might use it to buy my life. I see that I was right."

Hranna stood up, lodging the stick that Yansil had provided under her arm. She leaned toward her father, careful not to fall into the fire. She kissed him on the forehead. He stirred in his fitful sleep. She took a moment to study his face. Hranna wished she had Rolly's talent at drawing. Had things been different, she might have asked him for a likeness of her father. It was just one more way fate had been unkind. A plan had been forming in her mind, a way of gaining the wealth she still sought, and of protecting it as well. But if she failed, Hranna might never see her father again—not till their souls were made one with her mother in the ocean. There were times like these when the afterlife seemed so much more appealing than facing yet another impossible task.

Chapter 8

Hranna's eyes adjusted to the sunlight as she left the tent of meeting. The fire inside had been a source of comfort, like a home-cooked meal, which was something she intended to get before going back onto the ice. It was to be the last meal of the dying, apparently.

The fire inside the tent and the rigors of the past few days contributed to a profound distortion of Hranna's inner clock. Without the cycle of light and darkness, it was difficult enough to tell night from day. If she had been on the ice at this moment, Hranna might have remained clueless as to the time. Yet with a studied eye, she was able to get a close reckoning by merely surveying the village.

Their village contained at least a hundred families and an equivalent number of tents, yet very few people were moving around. She looked down the slope to the tents of the fishers and past their tents to the inlet where their small boats should be tied off. Only a few could be seen. So the fishers were still out on the ocean. Hranna looked up the slope to the tents of the hunters. From one or two of the tents, a thin tendril of smoke drifted from the contrived chimneys— the entrails of luftall stretched wide and thin in order to let the smoke out without letting the cold air in.

If she had to guess, Hranna would have to say it was very early in the morning in the village.

She rested a moment in the cold. Something she couldn't afford to do on the open ice. Knowing she was only a few steps from a fire created a sense of security. Hranna could appreciate why the other girls she had grown up with had chosen to tend fires rather than hunt or fish.

The familiar sounds of the village washed over her. In the background she perceived the susurration of the ocean's waves as they broke against the ice, raising and lowering the creaking boats. Hranna heard muffled conversations quieted by the earliness of the hour and the proximity of sleepers. She heard the clack of bone bowls as breakfast was prepared. She heard the ever-present crunch of footfall on the ice, something she missed on the hunt without ever knowing it. These were the sounds of a world without fear of imminent danger, a world of comfortable habitations and warm meals. It was the place of her birth, and she felt her connection to the village all the way through her feet down into the ice and the soil and the rock beneath.

It was really too bad that she would be leaving it all behind that very day.

Hranna thought about the items she would need for the task at hand, conscious always of the need to make what might be a long trip seem like a short run onto the ice. Supposedly she was going to retrieve Rolly's riches. She was sure that Inoah and his cronies like Yanka would be keeping a close watch on her preparations.

She intended to find Rolly's crew and seek their assistance in saving both him and, consequently, her as well.

Seeing as it was still early morning, Hranna went for the most necessary item first—breakfast. Walking up the hill, she saw that smoke was already coming from the chimney of her aunt's tent. She pulled the door flap back and quickly stepped in before any snow or cold air could follow. The impact of the cooking fire combined with the smell of a dozen or so sleeping bodies was overwhelming after being so isolated on the open ice. Yet it was not an altogether unpleasant scent. It was more like the smell of her father's furs at the end of the month, before they were washed. It was simply the smell of a warm and happy home. A happy tent was something Hranna had experienced indirectly by her connection to her aunt's large family. In contrast, Hranna was an only child and half-orphaned since she was nine years old. The tent of her mother's older sister had become like a second home to Hranna, and sometimes a better home than the original.

Hranna was greeted by a warm smile from her Aunt Gyurtuh who was tending the fire in the middle of the tent. A younger cousin, Hrite, was tending the chimney bladder. Hrite was the closest thing Hranna had to a friend in the village. The younger girl looked up to Hranna in an endearing way. The fact that they were as different as snow and water had never stopped them from playing together as children or whispering together through the long, cold nights as they grew up.

Hrite could barely spare her a smile now, busy as she was catching the smoke from the fire. Left unattended, the smoke might overwhelm the tent. Larger tents, like the one Hranna had just left, had large enough chimney bladders to catch the smoke easily without assistance. Smaller, family tents often required someone to chase down the smoke with the end of the bladder, allowing the hot air to push the smoke up and out the other end of the bladder that extended from the top of the tent.

Hranna caught an image in her mind of the round village tents each with a bladder leaking smoke from the top like a demon's nipple. She found it easy enough to return her aunt's smile.

A kind whisper greeted her. "Take off your fur, browen hunter."

Though she and Rolly must have arrived late in the night, Hranna was not surprised to learn that her aunt already knew of her exploits.

"And ice hunter of luftall," Hrite added quietly.

"Yes, and finder of strange, rich men on the ice. Wish to the ocean we were all so lucky." Her aunt always had a way of taking Hranna down a peg without diminishing her exploits. Hrite hid her smile with the back of a hand while chasing smoke with the other.

Hranna could practically hear what the young girl was thinking. She whispered back, "Nothing happened."

Aunt Gyurtuh's eyes glittered, "I heard they found your three legs practically entwined."

Hrite gasped. A sleeper stirred but did not rise. Hranna rolled her eyes. Only her aunt could joke so lightly about a crippling injury.

"Frostbite take the tongues of gossips." Hranna muttered a curse.

"Surely you wouldn't wish such a fate on your poor aunt?"

"Don't be so sure, old woman," said Hranna.

"Old woman, she calls me," said Gyurtuh looking meaningfully at her daughter, Hrite. "Not such an insult from the lips of an old maid."

Hranna felt a pang of anxiety fill her belly. In her own way, her aunt was asking about the conversation with Inoah that had taken place only moments earlier. The anxiety was not out of embarrassment for herself at being rejected but at the pain her aunt must feel for her when she revealed the rejection in its fullest implications. At least she could trust her aunt to grasp the nuances without having to spell them out.

"Inoah and I are not to be married. Nor am I likely to find a man soon who lives up to my high standards."

Her aunt stared into the cooking fire for a moment before nodding. One of the sleeping figures grunted and rolled over. It was probably one of Gyurtuh's restless boys fighting a luftall in his dreams.

"I know, Hranna." She looked over at her daughter. "Inoah has chosen our own dear Hrite."

The girl flew to Hranna before even surprise could reach her.

"Please forgive me, Hranna. How could I say no?"

With a knife to the throat? Hranna thought, but didn't say it out loud. This turn of events could not have been more disastrous. Hrite's father had been one of her father's staunchest supporters. If he had agreed to the marriage, things were much worse for Hranna and for her father than she suspected. This announcement would have taken the legs right out from under her, had one not already been pulled off by a thrashing luftall. Hranna had not been out hunting on the ice for long, barely a ten-day. Had so much changed in that time? Had she been so blind to developments in the village?

No, she thought. In the back of her mind, the part that made political calculations, she had known how things stood, even if her conscious mind was not ready to accept the new facts of life. After all, it was why she had made a mad attempt attacking a luftall on the open ice. Things really were that desperate for her.

She forced a smile and patted Hrite's hands which so tightly clasped her own.

So, Inoah would marry her cousin. It made a great deal of sense politically. Inoah would win the support of Hranna's uncle while tying himself even closer in bloodline to the old chief—though as a distant cousin himself, Inoah was practically family, as was everyone in the village really.

For Inoah, the match made sense. For Hranna, it was a calamity. And perhaps Inoah knew it. The friendship between Hrite and Hranna was no secret.

The support of a tent that had been like home to her was now gone. Her only friend turned against her. Well, not openly against her. Hrite cared for her still, but she was to marry Inoah. Things couldn't be the same between them. The poor girl might not have realized what was so obvious to Hranna.

A shadow passed over her aunt's face. As always, Gyurtuh understood. That was why Hranna had come to her aunt's tent—not only for a warm breakfast, she needed assistance, good advice, and a friendly ear. Yet how could Hranna tell her aunt just how cruelly Inoah had treated her—sending her back onto the ice in a way that would surely kill her? Would they see the design behind it, and had she any right to make them feel anger toward a future member of their family? Worse yet, would Hrite defend him?

How could she tell Hrite or her aunt about the desperate plan to find Rolly's people? She could not speak her mind in front of Hrite. A sense of loyalty to her future spouse might compel her to give away Hranna's secrets.

It was as if her aunt had handed her a bowl full of bitterness instead of her favorite dish: a steaming helping of luftall porridge mixed with tree leaves and dried salt from the sea. Normally the taste of her aunt's cooking was exquisite. Surely Gyurtuh had not changed her recipe. Then it must be Hranna's own mouth that betrayed her, drawing no flavor from the porridge. The warm porridge did nothing to smooth away the lump in her stomach. She congratulated her cousin, kissing her cheek. Hranna avoided her aunt's questioning looks, and, as soon as could be managed without being rude, Hranna left the tent, having never removed her outer furs.

Hranna felt well and truly alone. She leaned on the pole Yansil had given her and considered her next move. Working alone, her options were limited. She needed a new skisen and to repack her sled in a way that maintained the pretense of a day's trip across the ice. She also needed to visit Rolly one last time, to see if his condition had changed and to ensure he received proper care while she was away.

Aside from Inoah, Balras the hunter had the best skisen. He was one of the merriest men in the village. Hranna was glad it was his smiling face she would see next after such a disappointing visit with her aunt.

Hranna remembered that Balras had birthed a few young skisen last season that might have matured by now, if some other hunter hadn't beat her to them. She weighed in her mind whether she would take a male or a female.

A mixed set of skisen usually made the best team in her opinion, though the topic was a source of endless debate in the village. But to replace Nar with a young, male skisen so soon after losing him might create problems for Bin. Those two had been a pairing in the truest sense. A young male might not understand the situation, charged as all bucks were by the vigor of life.

If Balras had a suitable younger female, that might do nicely. It would mean sacrificing the ability to pull heavier weight. But Hranna did not intend to drag a luftall home this time. She was going on a much bigger hunt. Male skisen were good for heavy loads or short bursts of speed. Female skisen, given proper incentive, would run till their hearts burst.

So thinking, Hranna arrived at Balras's tent. The smoke of a breakfast fire drifted out of the tent's upper bladder. He was an old widower. His children had grown into families of their own. He lived now with his skisen. Hranna suspected he sometimes let them into the tent with him during the coldest nights.

Not wanting to interrupt his meal, Hranna skirted Balras's tent, approaching the adjoining stable. A low fence kept the skisen penned in. The hill rose sharply up, culminating in a lean-to that served as a shelter for the skisen. Not that they needed the shelter or the fence.

By the time a skisen was old enough to have jumped the fence, it was either already either too well trained to try it or had been put in a stew. They had no place for wild skisen in the village. Hranna considered the analogy to her own life. She was in the stew already. The next day or two would determine whether she would be cooked or not.

Hranna saw a short, straight horn sticking up in the midst of the skisen that milled about on the hill. She took from her pocket some tree leaves that she had liberated from Gyurtuh's pantry for this very purpose. She held a slender leaf over the fence rail and gave a short whistle.

The skisen eyed this new arrival at the gate. The adults, knowing that their own breakfast was a short time away, disdained the proffered leaf. But the young skisen, who were still a curious bunch, came over to investigate. Hranna handed the leaf to her first choice: a pretty young skisen with soft white fur. The young doe gratefully accepted the offering.

Hranna's hand recoiled. The doe's left eye was white as ice. The poor thing must be blind in that eye. Hranna offered her another bite. She wondered why this young female had not been harvested for its meat and its fur. Surely Balras did not intend to put her out onto the ice with only one eye. Hranna thanked the ocean that the browen's swipe hadn't taken Bin's vision.

Hranna looked over the other beasts. Balras had a young male that seemed promising. Had conditions been different, Hranna might have taken him.

"See something you like?"

Hranna hadn't heard Balras approach. He walked as quietly on the ice as the skisen he raised. It was a trick Hranna wished she knew and one she would have to be more on guard against as her life, at present, hung in the balance. She wouldn't put it past Yanka—no, perhaps not the waterwan—but she would not put it past one of Inoah's other acolytes to murder her in hopes of gaining the new chief's approval. Yanka seemed smart enough to know that even if Inoah appreciated the effort, he would immediately have the murderer executed in order to save face. Yet there was always one idiot in the bunch. Hranna determined to be more careful about who approached her.

"I didn't mean to disturb your meal," she said.

"A bachelor's table is easy to leave," said Balras. "Besides, the skisen told me you were out here waiting."

Hranna didn't know whether to believe Balras or not. He was always smiling and was often as silly as he was serious. It was not so unusual a trait as one might imagine in a people born to hardship.

"What about the older male?" said Balras, pointing up the hill.

At the suggestion, Hranna's shoulders immediately relaxed. She didn't know that she'd been carrying so much tension. Balras understood her situation and was making a sensible offer.

"I was thinking about a younger female."

"So was I," joked Balras. Hranna didn't laugh.

"Well, that might work, if I had one." Balras rubbed at a wispily bearded chin. He hadn't bothered with his

mittens. If he still had a wife, she would have reminded him. She also would have made him shave.

Balras buried his free hand deep into the fur of the
nearest skisen.

Hranna hunkered down in the snow. It was hard
to do with only one foot. She relied heavily on the
wooden pole Yansil loaned her. Balras removed his
hand from the warm fur and squatted in front of her.
The time had come to haggle.

Balras began the bargaining. "Trade me Bin, and
I'll give you the young buck and his mom for a good
price."

The offer took Hranna aback. She hadn't considered buying a whole new pair. But after what Bin had
done on the ice, sticking her horn into that browen
at the crucial moment, Hranna found that she just
couldn't bear to part with her.

"What about the young female?" Hranna waited to
see Balras's response to the one-eyed doe. He hadn't
counted her when Hranna had asked after a young
female.

"Moon? She's half blind."

Hranna's eyes narrowed ever so slightly at mention
of the young skisen's name. Was it fate?

"Why did you keep her?"

"She's a funny thing," Balras said. "She makes me
smile."

Hranna frowned. Her practical mind couldn't follow his reasoning.

"She's clever," he added. "She wasn't born blind. Got kicked in the face during birth by her own mama." Balras tilted his head to one side and shrugged, attributing the does deformity to the work of fate. "Thought I might breed her. Called her Moon cause it's what her eye looks like."

"I'll pay you three browen teeth for her."

"You're mad." Balras's smile grew even bigger.

"Too few?"

"Who are you going to breed her with?"

"I'm going to take her on the ice."

"I should pay you. I'll get free drinks off that joke for a week."

"I'm serious. You say she's clever?"

"Clever don't fix blind."

"Four teeth, then."

"By the ocean girl, have it your way. Pretty girls are always taking advantage of old Balras."

Hranna shook her head, smiling. The old man was nearly the same age as her father, though in better health.

She could not return his flirtation, but she thought there might be something she could give him besides—a joke he might appreciate. Remembering how Rolly had tried to seal their bargain, Hranna stuck out her hand. Balras examined it.

"Take it. It's how the blue man sealed our deal for the luftall."

"No kidding?"

"They touch gloves."

"What's the point?"

Hranna shrugged and started to rise. Balras took her mittened hand in his bare mitt of a fist.

"No one will believe it."

"Ask the blue man when he wakes?"

"He talks?"

"As clear as your skisen."

Balras slapped a hand on his leathered upper thigh. "The whole ocean, if you didn't inherit your father's sense of humor."

Hranna handed the browen teeth over to Balras.

"Any thoughts on how to drive skisen with one foot?"

Balras put a hand to his chin, taking on look of someone who had spent considerable time considering that very question.

"Hold on tight?" he suggested, smiling.

Hranna returned the smile and waited.

"I've heard it done before. You're not the first to go lame," he said. "Give me a ten-day, and I think I can rig you something."

"I'm leaving today."

Balras's smile faded. A cold breeze chose that moment to whip a smattering of loose snow between them. He didn't ask any questions. Hranna appreciated that. Nor did he accuse her of being crazy. Traveling the waste in her condition was so obviously mad that it wasn't worth saying. Balras must know that Hranna had her reasons and left her to them.

Inoah had given her a chance to live—at a price that might cost Hranna her life. She intended to improve on the bargain.

"You'll have to drive them by voice," he said finally. "Course you would have to anyway as I never trained Moon to run a sled on the ice. Never thought—" He let the idea trail off, its obviousness again not being worth the waste of breath.

***

Hranna arranged for the skisen to be delivered to the stable beside her father's tent. Balras would see that the young doe and Bin got to know each other. After all, he spoke skisen.

She had one last visit to make and this was the most difficult of the bunch.

Hranna walked back to the tent of meeting at the center of the village before striking out for the cliff that held Yansil's hut. The crutch hardly impaired her movement over the ice, though it sometimes sunk too far under her weight and had to be forcefully removed from the hole it created.

The healer lived on the edge of the village owing to the strange smells arising from the medicines that were part of her trade. Hranna had practically grown up on Yansil's foul-tasting teas, which were made from skisen horns, mistletoe, a variety of roots, and several secret ingredients. The women in the village swore by their medicinal properties. But they hadn't saved Hranna's mother. She hadn't tasted one of the bitter teas since.

As Hranna approached the small tent, the smell of boiling herbs caused her tongue to water in horrid anticipation. She could almost taste the high acrid tang in the back of her mouth. More than eight years had passed since her last draught, yet she could not convince her tongue that she had no intention of making it undergo that ordeal ever again.

"Yansil?" She stood at the door to the tent, calling the old woman's name. This was not a familiar place like Gyurtuh's where she might enter at a moment's notice uninvited, just as any other member of the family.

"Come." A faint reply reached her through the layered skins that formed the walls of the tent.

Hranna stooped as she entered. Like all of the tents, the ceiling ended about chest high. You could not stand inside a tent. Standing and working was done outside. One entered a tent only to rest or to eat. The remainder of life was spent out of doors. Hranna preferred the open air to the stifling environs of a tent, especially this tent with its cloistering scents.

Hranna nodded to Yansil, who was tending the cook fire at the center of the tent. Rolly lay on the far side of the tent. Hranna was secretly glad for that. Anyone who sought to harm him would have to move physically past Yansil as Hranna was now doing. Not that the old woman was a physical threat. But violations of her sanctum carried other deadly sanctions, such as a refusal to see one's child the next time it fell ill. Yansil had obviously chosen Rolly's placement on purpose. Hranna was grateful.

Hranna knelt beside Rolly. She examined the bearded face that had once been so animated. Now he lay pale but breathing under a layer of furs. She noticed that his lips were stained as was his beard. Yansil had been forcing her concoctions down his throat. Well, thought Hranna, they can't hurt and might well keep him hydrated. Though the body might go without food for some days, water was always a necessity.

Hranna placed her ear to Rolly's mouth. Her chest covered his. She listened for his breath. It came evenly as his chest rose and fell under hers. The scent of cut trees was only barely noticeable over the overwhelming smell of Yansil's tent.

The old healer might get the wrong idea from this display, but it was necessary to her plans. As Hranna checked his breath, she secretly pulled at the tab that closed the pocket over Rolly's belly. It rattled quietly as the pocket came open. Hranna found she was holding her own breath against the sound, fearful that Yansil would become curious.

Hranna slipped the moondial and the book out of Rolly's pocket and into the front of her own jacket. She closed the pocket as silently as she could before standing. Yansil's attention remained stuck to the boiling bowls of medicine. One hand held the chimney bladder, trying to trap and release as much of the rising fog as she could. Hranna wondered briefly whether the old woman liked the taste of her own medicine. She put the idea quickly out of her mind. The opposite, to Hranna, spoke of an unthinkable and unlivable life.

She would not end up like Yansil. She would die first out on the ice before she lived in a hut outside the village. As she knelt next to Rolly, she also found that she couldn't stomach the idea of betraying the man to Inoah, which is certainly what would happen if she gave Inoah Rolly's treasured pack full of metal. Inoah would have no further need of Rolly and had already argued, fairly successfully, that they ought to kill Rolly out of hand to prevent an invasion of strange men wearing blue coats. Hranna shook her head. Rolly said they had come to study the wastes. Some were even interested in studying her own people. It was a concept that perhaps only Yansil or maybe Balras could understand, those who had devoted their lives to understanding medicine or skisen. Despite his meditation, Yanka could not perceive the truth because the waterwan only received visions, he didn't pursue spiritual knowledge. Hranna realized that she too had made a sort of study of the creatures she hunted, noting their patterns and recording each hunt in her mind for future reference. Perhaps Inoah was the same but was blinded by playing at chief while her father ailed.

There was no use thinking about it any further. The situation was as solid as the ice beneath the snow. Only a profound shakeup might cause it to move. That might happen if she returned with a group of fire-shooting strangers. But she needed to be sure of Rolly's care first.

She slipped the metal pouch out of her pocket—the one that had contained Rolly's medicine—and put it into Yansil's hand.

"It's metal," said Hranna.

"I'm not blind."

"He used it like a flagon to hold liquid." Hranna demonstrated how the lid twisted to open and close. Yansil shook the pouch out into her hand. A few drops of liquid fell into her palm She licked them and grimaced.

"Tastes like medicine."

"I think you could rinse it out—"

"Why?"

"Because I'm giving it to you. Take care of him."

"I would anyway."

"Then I'll trade you for it. Two flagons full of luftall oil."

"I'll have some tea ready in a moment and a special potion you might try."

"No, just the luftall oil, thanks." Hranna had no intention of drinking whatever Yansil had mashed up. Rolly was lucky he was unconscious.

"Yansil, you won't let anyone. I mean till I return, you won't—"

"I'll do all I can, girl."

"I don't trust Yanka or one of the others not to—"

"That waterlogged old rat? You leave him to me."

The enmity Yanka held for Yansil was every bit reciprocated. Hranna used that knowledge to her advantage.

Hranna let the conversation drift off. Yansil didn't ask where Hranna was going or why she might be so concerned about Rolly. Such a direct question might be appropriate between close friends or family, but an acquaintance like Yansil would not be so blunt. She would be expected use intuition to divine meaning from the context of the conversation; or, more likely, she expected to hear all about it through gossip later.

Communicating through nuances and subtlety was a defensive mechanism among a people so few in number. It was one of the only ways to preserve the appearance of privacy.

From Hranna's display and questions about Rolly, Yansil would be expected to understand that she cared very much about him, perhaps loved him.

In all honesty, Hranna didn't know how she felt about Rolly. She certainly did not feel as strongly as the display to the old healer would imply. She assumed that the entirety of this conversation, absent mention of the priceless metal flagon, would reach Inoah's ears eventually. If he thought she felt more for Rolly than she did, he might hold the man hostage against Hranna's return with the treasure rather than sticking a horn through his heart the moment she left.

Nothing prevented the latter except the agreement they had made. And she had hardly been in the best bargaining position. If she had leverage, she wouldn't be preparing to risk her life going back onto the ice.

Hranna nodded, "Thanks for the pole." She used it for balance as she rose to leave.

Yansil handed her two flagons of luftall oil. She put a smaller bladder in Hranna's hand as well.

"Girl, take this as well."

Hranna looked at it with a raised eyebrow. If it was full of tea, it was going over the cliff as soon as she walked out the door.

As if the old healer could read Hranna's thoughts, she responded, "It isn't tea or a potion, though oceans know you could use it. I know you hate my tea. No," Yansil patted the bladder lightly. Hranna could feel the liquid shifting in the bag. "It's the urine from the browen you killed."

Hranna nearly dropped it.

"Careful," the old woman chastised Hranna. "That's very useful on the ice." Yansil turned her attention back to the fire and to tending the smoke bladder.

Hranna strained her imagination. Browen were fiercely territorial. Judicious use of the urine might discourage a browen, or a pack of wollen for that matter, from hunting her should they decide she was fair game, which, given her injuries, she probably was. If anything went wrong at all, If one of her skisen went lame, she would be a snack for some predator.

Enough, Hranna told herself. Thinking that way was bad luck, and she'd had enough bad luck the past few days to suspect there was a demon hanging around seeing what other mischief it might cause. Better not to give it any ideas.

She made her way out of Yansil's tent and down the small cliff as quickly as she could. All the better to get upwind of the smell. Rolly would never smell like trees again. He might not ever be able to scrub Yansil's scent out of his clothes or skin. He might even have to shave that beard. She wondered what he looked like underneath.

Hranna found herself outside the tent of meeting in the middle of the village. She stuck her head in to see if her father was still there. She had thoughts of telling him goodbye. Hranna knew she was only delaying the inevitable, but it seemed a right enough idea to justify a moment's dalliance.

Though the fire still burned, the chief no longer occupied the bench near it. He must have gone back to their tent. Hranna walked deeper into the tent of meeting. She remembered all that had happened here just as she remembered every hunt. She valued each of her father's political victories as much as every trophy she'd ever taken off a luftall. While the browen kill might have superseded even her father's best individual accomplishment as chief, overall, his rule had seen their village achieve an overarching peace and prosperity. That was certainly more valuable that one measly browen kill, however satisfying it might be and however much it might be sung of later. No one sang songs about basic civic virtue, but they should, she thought. They just didn't know how much effort it took to maintain peace. Certainly more effort than it took to kill a big luftall or the browen.

Would Inoah be able to maintain what her father had built? Hranna didn't know.

Casually she knocked one stool over, then another till they formed a small, uneven stack. She pushed her father's tall stool on top of the rest. Hranna emptied one of the flagons of luftall oil onto the pile. Finally, using her crutch, she turned the contents of the fire onto the wood. Hearing as well as seeing the familiar "whoosh" as the luftall oil on the stools caught fire.

Hranna limped out of the tent of meeting. Whatever else happened, Inoah wouldn't occupy her father's seat.

***

Hranna reached her father's tents with assistance from the crutch. He was not inside the main tent. He might be sleeping in his room.

Hranna resolved not to disturb him after all. She went to her room and collected her things, still roughly assembled from the previous trip. Catching her tent with Rolly's backpack up under her arm, she struggled awkwardly out of her tent. She did not look back or reminisce as she might have done were she in Gyurtuh's tent. There were as many bad memories as good in her old home.

Hranna made her way around the tent to the skisen stable in back. A glance at the tent of meeting showed that a bit more smoke than usual was rising from the chimney bladder. Hranna estimated that the entire structure would be on fire in a few short moments.

Balras was at the stable. He had Bin and the new skisen, Moon, attached to a sled. It wasn't Hranna's sled.

Balras smiled at her.

"It's something I've been working on."

Hranna stumped around it, examining the fine craftsmanship. It was a masterpiece of detailed wood-work.

There was a small stool mounted where she would normally stand. She tested it with her hand.

"I just added that seat because, you know," he said, motioning toward her leg.

Hranna examined the skisen herder's face. "Balras, I—"

"You paid too much for Moon." He patted the skisen's small head and rubbed her horn. She was obviously his favorite. "And I've been wanting someone to test my new design. Need someone crazy enough to do it. See?"

Balras bent toward the curved front of the runners. Hranna could see they were different somehow. They weren't flat like the runners on her old sled. These runners had deep grooves running down the center. How long it had taken to cut those grooves was beyond imagine.

"You take luftall oil, and you—" Balras helped himself to the full flagon that Hranna was carrying. She was glad he hadn't reached for the empty one.

That might have taken some explaining. Instead, she watched as he poured a little of the oil into the groove at the top of each runner.

"See, as the oil goes down the groove—well, it makes the sled go faster." He stood up, beaming at his handiwork. Hranna didn't bother to point out that, if recent experience was any proof, leaving a trail of luftall oil on the ice might paint a big fat line for a browen to follow.

She needed speed. Even if he had told her it ran on Yansil's tea, she wouldn't have turned it down.

Hranna stowed her gear and mounted the sled. The stool felt good underneath her. It might actually beat having to stand while driving a team, and certainly was an improvement in this instance since she couldn't guide this team by subtle shifts in weight. She lashed her crutch to the runner.

Balras held out his hand. "I think this merits a touch of the gloves."

It really did. Hranna shook his hand.

"Balras—"

"Oh, you don't have to thank me, girl. How long have we known each other."

"No, Balras," she faltered, "I mean, thanks, yes, but," Hranna pointed over the man's shoulder, "the tent of meeting is on fire."

As Balras turned to look, a cry rose up. Someone else had spotted the plumes of smoke rising out of the tent. Hranna saw villagers rushing toward the doomed edifice. Balras himself took a few steps toward the tent and began to bark out orders as though he was commanding skisen.

"Hyop!" Hranna told Bin to pull out. She put the blaze to her back and drove out of the village. The runners on the new sled slid over the ice like a fisherman's boat on a smooth ocean. She might succeed on her crazy mission or she might fail. Either way, she was going to do it fast.

Chapter 9

Hranna examined the drawings in Rolly's book. She was standing on the hill where they had confronted the browen. Its frozen corpse lay just down the slope. Hranna had carved off as much of the remaining meat as she could. It was a good thing she had the sharp, metal knife from her father. Using bone tools would have been impossible for her in her physical state. Her arm was still a mess from where Rolly stabbed her. And she had difficulty maintaining her balance on one leg. Her new condition was going to take some getting used to, provided she lived long enough to master the skill of walking with the crutch.

She paged through the book, looking for a familiar landmark. She could not read the scratches Rolly had made. Perhaps they were important or even critical. It didn't matter now. She would have to trust the drawings themselves. Thankfully Rolly was a decent artist.

There. She saw an image of the rocky outcropping near the luftall's cliff. She flipped a few pages back, careful not to bend or tear the fragile leafs. She soon found an image of the drift where they had first met. Hranna thought she could find that place easily enough if she simply backtracked from the hill on which she was standing.

She was going to find Rolly's people. That was her genius plan. And afterward? She hadn't a clue. She would improvise as always. In the back of her mind, she was envisioning a group armed with Rolly's red stars versus the sticks and horns of her village. It was a force she could use to keep the metal she had bargained for and to turn negotiations with Inoah back in her favor. It was crazy. Would they listen to her? She hoped that they would once she explained, with a little exaggeration, the danger that Rolly was facing.

She turned to the next page. There was the image of a beautiful woman. A lump instantly lodged in Hranna's throat. Her hand went to her ear. Hranna hadn't imagined that she was the first woman Rolly had drawn, nor had she thought that she cared. Yet, looking at the foreign goddess on the page made her feel all the roughness of her life on the ice. She couldn't tell the color of the woman's eyes or hair from the charcoal drawing. Hranna imagined she was as fair as Rolly with the same light blue eyes. The woman's smile was coy. Around the crown of her head ran a thin line that might be some kind of adornment. The necklace that graced her neck was most certainly made of metal carved in intricate patterns. An inscription ran beneath the image, but Hranna could not read it.

Hranna resisted the urge to tear out the page. She turned it carefully instead and was glad she had not given in to emotion, for on the back of it, extending to the other page, was the next formation she must seek if she was to find Rolly's lost team.

Hranna didn't recognize the formation. Then again, everything looked so similar on the ice. Thankfully a large storm had not arisen that would shift the landscape. She memorized the image.

Hranna slipped the moondial out of her pocket. She hadn't had to take it. She didn't want it falling into Inoah's hands if he decided to search the stranger, as he certainly would do at some point.

Hranna opened the dial as she'd seen Rolly do so many times. What she saw took her by surprise. The top remained attached to the bottom by way of a flexible metal ligament. The top stood straight up in the air. Inside the top was a piece of metal as reflective as a becalmed ocean. Hranna could see her own face in it as clearly as the image Rolly had drawn for her. In fact, had she not seen the drawing she might have wondered just who was staring back at her from inside this strange device.

Inside the moondial, what looked like a sharp piece of bone was balanced on the end of a small rod. It vibrated at the least movement, but it did not spin on the rod as the wind flag had done. Hranna pulled a hand free from a mitten. She reached down to touch the bone. Her finger stopped just short of the object, blocked by some obstruction. Hranna examined the moondial from the side. The thinnest layer of what looked like clear ice blocked her. The extent of Rolly's magic never ceased to amaze her.

She gave up on the dial and focused on the image reflected in the moondial's open lid.

Hranna smiled and the image of Hranna smiled back. Hranna removed her hood, examining her mangled ear more closely. In the image, it didn't look as awful as she'd always imagined it in her mind. In fact, the triangular cut wasn't disfiguring. Had her hair not been so tightly braided, she might not even be able to see the cut. What had she been ashamed of all these years? Her practical mind had always said it was a silly thing to brood over, and here was proof. Hranna examined her ear again, bending it this way and that.

She caught movement in the image. Something small disappeared behind her head. Hranna turned to look. Three sleds were on the horizon. They were heading in her direction, traveling fast.

Hranna stuck the book and the moondial back into her front pouch. She sat down on her sled. "Hyop, Hyop!" She set Bin at a trot. The younger skisen followed the older female's lead.

Burning the tent of meeting had been a distraction. True, it had been cathartic. But it was mostly a means to ensure that, when Inoah had her followed, she would have a good lead on her pursuers. The plan had worked. She hadn't seen any sign of pursuit at first.

Now they were on her track. Hranna couldn't tell who it was at that distance. Maybe Rolly had some magic device of far-sight in his pack, but Hranna wasn't stopping to find out.

It was time to learn whether her bargain with Balras had been a good one. Hranna was certain—well, fairly certain—that nobody else was driving a team of female skisen. Most hunters preferred a male-female pairing or two males.

While a team of male skisen could run faster for short distances, Hranna had gambled that, on an extended chase, like the one she was about to lead these three on, having the endurance of a pair of female skisen might win the day.

Hranna reviewed her liabilities. Moon hadn't been out on the ice; hadn't built up her strength. But the young female had the energy and resilience of youth. Too, Hranna was weighed down with the browen meat. The other sleds were probably running light. Yet even that might work to her advantage. They might not have prepared for a several day chase across the ice.

She had Balras's sled. There wasn't another like it in the village. It was light and quick and ran smooth. Leaning precariously over the front, Hranna dropped a few more dollops of luftall oil into grooves in the runners even as she sent a few more prayers toward the ocean.

If she did lose those following her, she worried about what Inoah would do to Rolly once they returned with news of her disappearance. She was trusting that the deal she had made with Inoah might stay his hand. If he believed she loved the blue man, he might hold Rolly hostage against her return.

First things first. She had no intention of leading her pursuers to Rolly's people. Dramatic as it might be to ride into camp being pursued by armed men, her plan was tenuous enough without adding further complications.

As her team set into a rhythm on the ice, Hranna considered her options. This was not a short, sprinting race with an exciting ending. It was a race that would span hours, maybe days. If they ever got within striking distance of her, she would be done. Hranna had to keep them as far back as possible and, ultimately, to lose them. How then to lose experienced hunters on the open ice?

She let her mind wander over the landscape of the waste that she knew as clearly as her father's own face. The trick, as she saw it, was to get off the open ice. Hranna called out to Bin to alter course. She looped away from her destination, the place where she and Rolly had first met.

As happened so often on a hunt, Hranna began to see the rough outlines of a plan forming. She would lose them in the glaciers.

Knowing it would take some time before the terrain changed, Hranna worked on a contingency plan. As Rolly had pointed out on the cliff before they confronted the luftall, it was good to have a backup.

She pulled out the remaining browen teeth, examining the sharpened points in her mittened hand. They were small and sharp. She had traded the biggest and best to Balras for Moon. These would still do for the purpose she had in mind.

***

Walls of azure blue rose up in front of Hranna. The tips of the glaciers shot high above her head, forming at a distance what looked like a rolling wave of frozen souls, longing to reconnect with the ocean. Up close, the glaciers seemed like a series of impenetrable mountains. Looks could be deceiving. A circuit of narrow caves ran among and through the glaciers. Hranna hoped to lose her pursuers in this maze.

As with the wastes, she carried a rough map of the caves in her mind. Occasionally the map changed as she discovered that a cave-in had closed one tunnel or opened another. Hranna expected that the hunters who were tracking her were also familiar with the glaciers. But they would not know which route she would take or where she would emerge. The floors of the caves were not like the snowy waste outside. She would leave little evidence of her passage. If they guessed wrongly about her exit, they would be forced to ride the width of the glaciers to pick up her trail.

Hranna considered waiting in the caves for them to pass and going back the way she had come, but she did not have time for such games. Rolly's people were hard up for food. Rolly's own life would be in danger with every passing day. Hranna couldn't risk a game of hide and seek.

That wasn't to say she couldn't have a bit of fun at their expense. Hranna chose the narrow opening of a glacial cave. It did not lead directly to the exit she planned on taking, but that might throw off the trackers as well, provided they were able to get their skisen to enter the network of tunnels in the first place.

Hranna smiled. She called for Bin to slow down. The animal gladly complied. Moon followed Bin's example. So far, they had been working nicely as a team. Hranna speculated that the loss of half her sight might have forced Moon to be extra reliant on Bin.

As they reached the cave's mouth, Hranna called a halt. She touched the smooth sides of the blue tunnel. The contours were fascinating. She could see deep into the walls themselves.

Hranna reached into the sled and removed the bottles Yansil had given her. Out of one she took a drink of luftall oil. When she opened the other, her skisen gave a start. Bin's head and tail shot into the air almost piercing the roof of the cave with her sharp, straight horn. Moon's head was on the swivel. She was a clever beast. Clever enough to know the smell of browen urine.

"Hro!" Hranna called to settle them.

Hranna turned on her stool till she was facing the back of the sled. She took the round bladder in her good hand. The scent of concentrated, day-old browen urine filled the cave. No wonder Bin and Moon were stamping and snorting. If Hranna could smell the stuff, then, to their sensitive noses, it must seem like a browen was right behind them.

Hranna squeezed the top of the bladder so as not to spill the contents directly onto the ice. She shook it around the opening to the cave, splattering it onto the sides of the walls. She had never seen a browen mark its territory, but Hranna supposed she had done a half-decent job of it from the way her skisen were stamping, ready to bolt. Only their intensive training and Bin's connection to Hranna kept the sled in place. Moon, with only one good eye, must be twice as worried.

Hranna tied off the bladder, holding the remaining browen piss in reserve. "Hyop!" Her head jerked back as the skisen moved eagerly into the tunnel. Normally Nar and Bin had required a little coaxing to go among the glaciers. Hranna suspected that browen urine might be a good thing to take on the ice should one need to coax a little more speed out of a team.

Yansil might have more back in her hut. With a shudder, Hranna wondered what exactly Yansil did with the foul smelling liquid and just how much browen urine Hranna had unwittingly drank in Yansil's tea. The thought sent a spasm down into her belly. Apart from the meal at her Aunt's tent, she'd been surviving on luftall oil and bits of dried jerky over the past few days. Hranna felt the lack of food and the lack of sleep.

Hranna slowed the skisen down to a slow walk as they traversed the glacial tunnels. The perennial sun shone through the glaciers, sending sunlight through the blue ice, washing everything in a turquoise glow. The white fur of the skisen looked as though it had been dyed in the clearest depths of the ocean. Seated on the sled, wrapped in fur, Hranna had the chance to examine the caves above her. They were not uniform in appearance; the walls and ceiling flowed like the ocean. As they moved into an open gallery, her skisen team chose a path through columns of ice that were wide at the top and narrow in the middle. She let the beasts have their heads, only correcting them when it was necessary to choose a specific tunnel. Hranna was taking a circuitous path through the glaciers. It might have been better to rush from one end to the other, taking the most direct route out of the caves. However, that is what the hunters might expect, and if they chose to act on their hunch, they would emerge from the glaciers without the sight of her tracks in front of them. They would have to navigate around the glaciers till they found the opening where her tracks emerged.

She was heading for the cave opening closest to the place where she and Rolly first met. The hunters could not anticipate where she was going. Besides, after several days of pushing herself to her physical limit, Hranna was not in a hurry to leave the peaceful caves. Her arm ached where Rolly had gored it with the luftall tusk. Her leg felt weird as though she still had a foot.

They entered a tunnel where the walls resembled long drapes of fur fabric arranged artfully, cascading from an opening in the ceiling above, through which water must once have flowed. The blue light, the rhythmic fall of the skisen's padded hooves on ice, the warm blankets around her legs; these were all such calming comforts. Hranna's eyes closed. She forced them open, vaguely aware of the dangers of closing them out on the ice and while being chased inside a glacier. Hranna fought sleep. Shadows flickered in the corners of her eyes. They were the shape of a man in blue clothing. Tunnel openings doubled in her vision. She had to squint them back down to a single entrance. In the back of her mind, Hranna screamed to stay awake. Sleep on the ice meant death. Her body simply wouldn't listen. The long tunnels narrowed in her vision, fading from a quiet blue to a welcome gray as her eyes slid shut.

Chapter 10

Hranna awoke under the bluest of skies. Her eyes fought to focus on the rolling clouds. They looked close enough to touch. Hranna reached out a gloved hand. It stopped short. A barrier separated her from the clouds. It wasn't fair, she thought, to be near enough to plunge through them like a snow drift and yet be denied. Hranna's mitten remained on the barrier, probing for an opening. Her hand grew cold. The realization came sluggishly, that she was not among the clouds. Hranna was in a glacial tunnel, looking up at the sun through the ice. The clouds were patches of frost obscuring the otherwise clear ceiling.

A skisen snorted. Hranna leaned forward. She saw Bin and Nar—no, Hranna shook her head; it was Moon now, standing silently in the small cave. They were not moving. That was bad news. She had fallen asleep. Panic should be rising in her chest, but it wasn't. Her eyes blinked, eager to return to sleep.

Hranna reached slowly under her fur coverings. She drew the flagon of luftall oil to her mouth. Her lips couldn't feel the edge of the bottle, though she knew it had to be in the right place. She tilted it up. Hranna's tongue registered the salty taste. Her brain started working.

When the familiar warm glow of the oil hit her fingers and her remaining toes, Hranna came fully awake.

She had fallen asleep in the glaciers. She should be dead, her soul swimming in the ocean. But she wasn't. Hranna looked around. The tunnel was narrow and the passage in front had fallen in. The natural enclosure must have afforded her an amount of protection from the cold, sort of like Rolly's wollen hole. The ice above her head and near the skisen was stippled where condensation from their breath had formed and frozen again. Hranna drank some more of the luftall oil. It spread throughout her body but did not reach her nose or lips.

Hranna put a mittened hand to her face. She couldn't feel her nose, mouth, or eyebrows. She took off the mitten and tried again with a bare hand. Her face felt as cold as an ice statue. It was strange. Her skin felt like skin under her fingers, but because there was no corresponding feeling in her face, it almost felt as though she was touching someone else's skin.

Hranna knew the dangers of frostbite. She knew villagers who had stayed on the ice too long, till their outermost extremities turned traitor, forming a connection with the ice rather than their masters. Several villagers had lost a finger, foot, or even a nose that way.

Her hand traveled up her head. The skin under her hood was fine. Her damaged ear felt the same as always. If she had to lose an extremity, she would have preferred that the ice finish the job on that ear and not take her nose.

Still, there was some chance that feeling would return. Besides, she had never been a vain person. And if she was forbidden to marry, it might not really matter if her face was the type that would scare little children.

Hranna took a moment to spread luftall oil over her numb face before returning her hand to the mitten. Yansil might have a remedy for frostbite. Hranna wondered if it included browen urine. She still had a small bag of the stuff. There was no way she was going to apply that nasty, yellow wash to her face by way of experiment.

In her imagination or perhaps in real-life, Hranna thought she felt a tingle on the tip of her nose, signaling that the potent luftall oil was doing its work. Only time would tell. She didn't know how much time she had wasted in sleep. Nor did Hranna know where her skisen had wandered in the caves. She was lost.

***

None of the caves looked familiar. Normally, Hranna could have been led blindfolded to any place on the wastes and she would have found her way automatically—simple as knowing up from down. But the past few days had played havoc with her senses. She had no knowledge of time. And she no longer knew up from down. Rather, she had the sense that she was constantly falling.

Finally, Hranna entered the gallery with the tall ice columns. This one was unmistakable.

"Hro." She slowed Bin and Moon as they entered the huge cavern. She needed to be sure that she took the correct tunnel.

The pair stopped. But the noise of the sled, the harness and rigging, echoed through the chamber, as did the skisen's impatient snorts.

"Hush," she ordered them.

Bin looked back, giving Hranna an accusatory stare, as if to say that she was being quiet.

Hranna spied the source of the noise. Her eyes widened as three sleds spread out among the ice columns in front of her and sped toward her position.

Hranna chose a cave. She urged Bin toward it, calling out a constant stream of orders. She was at a disadvantage, not being able to guide the sled silently with her weight. But she did not intend to simply give up and let these three take her. Hranna unsheathed her knife.

She had gotten a good look at their rigs as she turned to sprint for the tunnel. Two of them were cousins closer to Inoah's side of the family. In front of them was Inae, Hrite's younger brother. Hranna didn't even know that Inae had his own sled.

He was moving fast. The curved horns of his skisen pumped as they raced toward her. Inae was angling to cut her off.

He was going to reach her before she gained the safety of the tunnel. He was just a few columns away. Hranna grabbed the bottle of browen urine. She stabbed the side with her knife. No time to open it. Hranna lobbed the small sack at the feet of Inae's on-rushing skisen. It burst on the ice.

The skisen panicked. Her team put on speed. Inae's team reeled. Unable to stop quickly on the icy floor, they skidded, sending his sled into the side of a column. Inae shot over the front of the sled and skidded to a stop in a heap. Hranna winced. Inae was like family to her. She fought the urge to go to him. Even as she decided against it, she saw Inae move, sitting himself up on the ice. He would live. Hranna breathed a sigh of relief that was almost stolen from her lungs as they plunged into a small opening in the cavern wall.

One of the cousins followed close after her.

"Hro!" Fighting the urge to panic, Hranna told her team to slow down. She knew these caves. They would travel for some time before the cave opened up enough to let a sled pass, bringing weapons to bear. There was no sense tiring her team. She would need every ounce of their strength if she were to escape.

Hranna could almost feel the warm breath of the pursuing skisen as they came up behind her.

"Hranna!" The lead rider called to her.

"Who is it?"

"Anarra and my brother Amrak behind me."

"And Inae too?"

"That frostling? The cub wanted to run with the bucks."

Frostling, was it? A rider as fresh as the first frost. The moniker certainly applied to Inae. It might indeed be his first time on the wastes without his father or older brothers.

Yet the revelation was interesting. It meant that Inae might not be aware of the real purpose of the hunter's mission. She almost felt bad about busting up his sled.

Anarra's skisen came in close behind her. Hranna sensed the threat. Turning in her seat to face the skisen, Hranna hefted her hunting pole in her hands.

"Back off. I'll take an eye before they ever lay a horn on me."

The team dropped back a few steps. Hranna continued to face backwards. Rolly had been right. They needed distance weapons. Of course, if they had such weapons, Hranna would be the one at a disadvantage. If she survived, though, Hranna thought she might revisit the idea. This whole killing each other in close quarters was okay for the occasional battle between villages. It ensured that not too many of their already small numbers were killed at once. Yet, even with her limited imagination, Hranna could envision a situation where the quick destruction of a dangerous village might be a good thing.

"Come back with us, Hranna," Anarra called down the tunnel.

"Not likely. I'm not going to help Inoah kill me."

"He wouldn't."

"He told you that? You think I'd risk my life running out onto the ice otherwise?"

Anarra was silent for a moment. "Come on. We know these caves as well as you. We're going to catch you."

He was probably right. But she had a few more tricks. In the last three days she had killed a luftall on the open ice and a browen. Hranna was not going without a fight.

There was nothing more to say to Anarra. Hranna did not return any further remarks. Eventually, Anarra fell to joking with his brother behind him. Hranna could hear them plainly enough, but it was nothing worth listening to. It was the same sort of chatter one always heard on a hunt. They were acting like they were out for a simple stroll on the ice.

Hranna spent the time preparing. She cut a thin tendon off of the browen meat. She shoved the remaining browen teeth and claws into the strip before paring it down into several small segments. She was holding a small fortune in her hands. Her life was worth more.

Hranna sensed the narrow tunnel was coming to an end. It would soon open up into a series of broader tunnels. Anarra would be able to come alongside her. His male skisen could outrun Bin and Moon in a sprint. He could easily overpower her or kill her if that was his true design. It was time to make her move. Unfortunately, she couldn't disguise it from her pursuers.

"Hyop! Hyop!"

"She's making a run!" Anarra said to his brother.

Hranna's sled picked up speed. There was no snow underfoot to slow it down. Her skisens padded feet were sure on the ice. Unfortunately, so were Anarra's. He kept pace with her easily. His skisen's curved horns pumped uncomfortably close.

Hranna turned on her stool again.

"Just let me go, Anarra."

"Not a chance."

Hranna dropped the tendon strips. They bounced on the ice and under the onrushing feet of Anarra's skisen. The teeth of the browen and its sharp claws bit into the skisen's soft feet. They were running on solid ice, running hard, without any concern about the sureness of their footing. Every step of the male skisens was heavy. These heavy steps fell onto the sharp tendon strips, driving them deep into the skisen's tender feet. Not every strip found purchase, but Hranna knew sufficient damage would be done to bring them up lame for a time. Anarra would be walking home.

The skisen faltered. They bellowed in pain. The sled shuddered as they pulled up short. Hranna, still sitting backwards, gave a little wave goodbye. Anarra's eyes went wide as she pulled away. He had been leaning hard on the sled, urging his skisen forward by shifting his weight. The sudden stop threw him off balance. He leaned forward, then, overcompensating, fell back as his skisen stopped.

To Hranna, his fall happened slowly. She could see it happening but was powerless to help. Her hand was still held stupidly in the air. A skisen horn punched through Anarra's chest. Blood flew from his lips. He had fallen back into his brother's team. Amrak hadn't been able to react quickly enough to Anarra's sudden halt. Anarra's head fell back on impact. His eyes rolled into the back of his head.

He was dead or dying. Hranna was sure. An instant death would have been a blessing. His skisen were lame and blocking the tunnel. Anarra was trapped between his sled and his brother's skisen. There was no way for Amrak to reach him in that narrow tunnel.

Hranna felt the sick taste of bile rise in her throat. Amrak would never be able to prompt his brother's injured skisen into the wider cave ahead. He would have to move backwards, dragging his brother's dying body till they reached the cavern full of ice columns. It was a messed up and bloody business.

She hadn't wanted that to happen, hadn't meant to harm them. After all, they were family, however distant. Now, Anarra was dead and Amrak would want revenge. Inoah might let him have it.

Hranna set her jaw tight. Had they succeeded in capturing her, both her life and Rolly's would have been forfeit. It had been her life or theirs.

Hranna guided Bin and Moon through the network of caves, heading toward the chosen exit. She had avoided the pursuit and should be able to make her way to Rolly's people unmolested, but at the cost of the life of one of her own villagers.

***

Beautiful as the caves may be, they were too confined for someone used to life on the wastes. She breathed a great sigh of relief as they emerged from the glacial caves into the open sky.

That sigh was cut short by the sight of movement as Inae emerged from a tunnel farther down the glacier wall. She thought he was out of the running. Maybe his sled hadn't been as banged up as she'd imagined.

Hranna saw him lean forward, angling his sled toward hers. She still had a half-decent lead if she acted quickly.

Hranna called to Bin, setting the pair of skisen back into a run. Hranna hadn't wanted to make a close race out of this trip, but she would run her skisen to their death and hers before she'd be taken back to the village.

Hranna plowed over the snow, heading to the place where she had first spied Rolly and the moondial. Inae fell in far behind her, but still too close for comfort.

Chapter 11

The race was not as exciting as Hranna had imagined it would be when she first emerged from the glaciers. She thought Inae's male team would quickly catch her two smaller skisen. Yet Inae had gained little ground on her as she approached the snow drift where she and Rolly had first met.

She remembered being woken by Nar's cries as he first battled the browen and being half dragged out of her tent by Bin. That tent was now packed into the sled. She hadn't had time to repair it properly. Rolly's backpack was rolled tightly inside it.

Hranna looked over her shoulder. There was no way she was going to get to use the tent, not with Inae following so closely behind. She didn't even dare let her skisen rest or forage for food. Hranna took an occasional drink of luftall oil, but Bin and Moon hadn't rested or taken any food since their trek had begun. Thankfully, skisen were hearty creatures that, if pressed, could travel for long distances, days at a time, without complaining. People like Balras had bred them that way.

As she crested the top of the snow drift, Hranna slowed her skisen. She looked for the landmark Rolly had drawn in his book. Normally at this time of night, the landscape would be utterly dark. Now she could see clearly, exactly as Rolly had seen when he made his sketch. Hranna turned on her stool looking for the familiar lines from the drawing.

Hranna cursed the bad luck demon that had been her constant companion of late. Rolly's drawing was a perfect match for the nearest glacial peak. The next point on his cryptic map lay directly behind her. In the same direction as Inae.

She would have to make a wide circle if she wanted to maintain her lead. There just wasn't time. And her skisen didn't have the energy.

Hranna circled round the snow drift. She headed directly toward Inae.

If the young man was surprised, he did nothing to show it. His team never slackened their pace. The two sleds moved slowly together. Hranna busied herself, taking out the makeshift bowl that she used for cooking food on the ice.

She was close enough to see what Inae was wearing, borrowed furs that covered him like a poorly formed tent.

Hranna took a drink of luftall oil before pouring the contents of the flagon into the bowl.

Inae slowed down as they neared. Hranna didn't. She wondered what he was thinking. He must be preparing to turn and give chase.

Hranna concentrated on the bowl; she took out her knife and scraped it against a black rock, sending a spark down into the bowl. Immediately the luftall oil gave a little whoof, springing to life.

As they approached each other, Inae waved her down. He wanted her to stop. Again, not likely. He must not have known what happened to Anarra. Inae must have taken a different tunnel out of the glaciers, making up the time difference while Hranna plodded down the narrow tunnel before that long desperate race that had ended so tragically for Anarra and Amrak.

As Inae passed her, Hranna could see his face. He seemed so sincere in his desire to speak to her. Hranna calculated whether she could defend herself physically if she stopped—not while missing a foot and with a busted up arm. She just couldn't risk stopping.

But she saw no reason not to let Inae pull alongside. After all, his skisen should be able to outrun hers in a short race. She wondered why he hadn't caught her already.

Her curiosity was soon sated. The runners of Inae's sled were bent inward. It must have happened when his sled hit the ice column inside the cavern. There was no way his rig was going anywhere fast, however strong his team might be.

Hranna slowed as Inae made a tight turn.

He came up beside her, matching her pace.

"I'm glad you came back, Hranna."

With the enthusiasm of a young male, Inae mistook Hranna's silence as an opportunity to say whatever came into his head.

"Mother was so worried when you left. She sent me to find you. Gave me Dad's old sled."

That explained where he got the ride from. He might have borrowed the jacket too from the way it swallowed his torso. Maybe he'd inherited it from one of his older brothers.

"Did she say why I left?"

Inae blushed. "She said you had a disagreement with Inoah."

"That's one way to put it." If she were any closer to him, she would have tousled his hair as she had so many times. He was so infuriatingly like a younger brother.

Inae blurted, "I heard you talking this morning. He's not the only man in the village you know!" He quickly turned his face to the side.

Hranna rocked back. Thankfully her skisen weren't responding to her weight. So, not exactly like a little brother then—at least not from his perspective.

So, he had been the one who was awake when she spoke with Gyurtuh. Hranna remembered the sleeper who had grunted and rolled as if fighting a luftall. It must have been Inae.

Hranna raised one eyebrow. The fact that her face was responding on command was actually pretty encouraging. Hranna put a mittened hand to her cheeks. Feeling was definitely returning after the frosty nap inside the glacier. But Hranna knew from experience that when it did return in full, there'd be a lot of pain to deal with from where it had frozen.

Inae looked away. "I mean," he paused.

"Go home, Inae." She might have killed him and been well within her rights for making such an unwanted pass, flattering though it was.

"No."

"Go home. You can't help me."

Inae was barely sixteen years old. His apparent crush on her was kind of sweet, but she couldn't take care of anyone else, especially one so inexperienced on the ice.

"Last chance, Inae. Go home."

He set his face, determined. Hranna wasn't sure just how he intended to stop her. He didn't look sure himself.

Their sleds were close now, close enough to hold hands had she reciprocated Inae's feelings.

Hranna leaned over. Inae looked surprised but obviously pleased by her nearness.

She dumped the flaming luftall oil over the front of his sled, covering his tent and gear, catching fire to part of his jacket, engulfing the top of the runners. Everything, including Inae, was suddenly on fire.

"Sorry," said Hranna.

It was the second time she'd ruined his sled that day. And she really was sorry about it.

His sled jerked to a stop as he jumped off, removing his weight and all it communicated to his skisen. They stopped and looked around dumbly. If they caught sight of the fire, thought Hranna, they could bolt, leaving him stranded on the ice.

Hranna watched as he frantically rolled. Coming up smoking but no longer on fire, Inae scooped snow over the sled. Not good to use water on a grease fire, thought Hranna. Didn't your mother teach you that?

Finally the young man got wise. Pulling out his burning tent, he buried the flame in the snow before using the singed fabric to smother the rest of the fire.

Hranna could practically see the look of heartbreak on his face. She wasn't sure if he was more upset about losing her or about losing his first sled. Probably some weird combination of the two.

The glaciers loomed back up in front of Hranna. She would make it there, take a new bearing from the drawings in the book, and find Rolly's people.

She took one last look at Inae as he disappeared from view. Her jaw dropped. Another good sign of recovery from frostbite. Inae had managed to rehitch his sled and was still following in her tracks. She imagined he was pretty mad. If he ever caught up to her, there was going to be one awkward conversation.

Chapter 12

Hranna sat stiffly on the wooden seat of her sled. Bin and Moon pulled well enough. The sled moved smoothly and quickly over the ice. But they had all been at it a long time. Hranna longed to slide off the sled, to stand up for a moment. She wanted to stretch her cramped muscles. Bin and Moon needed a chance to forage. Hranna looked back over her shoulder.

An exasperated sigh passed Hranna's lips. Inae was still following them, stubborn as the first frost.

She turned back to Rolly's book. They had long ago passed by the first glacier. Hranna half expected Amrak to be waiting for her outside the glacier caves. She would never forget the look of shock and pain on his brother, Anarra's, face as the skisen horn punched through his chest. Hranna doubted Amrak was likely to forget it either.

Hranna blinked away the image. The drawings on the pages of Rolly's journal were leading Hranna toward the ocean. Given the general direction, Hranna guessed that Rolly's people were out on the ice floes. There was a frozen stretch of the great river that fed the ocean. It ran alongside the glaciers. On days when the moon disappeared, when the ice grew so cold, the river often froze. Anyone foolish enough to travel up that river at this time of year deserved any trouble they encountered.

Hranna flipped the page. There were only two pictures left in the book. She was riding hard toward the first. It was a jagged crust of ice and rock that stuck up out of the snow. In the drawing, the sun hung over its shoulder. The sun was not there now. It reeled through the sky like an early drunk, never staying in one place, sometimes falling, yet never managing to have sense enough to stay down.

She supposed that beyond the last drawing in the book, it would be obvious just where the party was camped. Hopefully Rolly hadn't forgotten anything crucial or, worse, written it in his indecipherable scrawl rather than drawing it like a normal, civilized person.

Hranna smiled. She had once thought that drawings, carvings, or a tale sung round the fire of gathering was the height of culture. How much more might they accomplish if her people could make a recording of their words and thoughts as Rolly did.

They would have to be careful how they used such a skill, of course. In such a tight community, your mind was the only place you could hide. Perhaps it was not better to record everything one thought.

Hranna certainly couldn't have recorded her thoughts on arriving at the jagged crust drawn in the book. The words running through her mind would have set the paper on fire, as hot as any spark put to luftall oil.

The crusted outcropping of rock marked the edge of a small cliff that let down onto the frozen river. Hranna hadn't even known it was there. Of course, it had to be there. The river did not run at the same level as the ice around it. There must be a bank.

The edges were not as steep as the cliffs beneath which the luftall lay. The sides of the cliff sloped down onto the river at an angle soft enough to get the sled down but hard enough to make her think twice about trying to ride it. The smart thing to do would be to port the sled and its contents to the bottom of the slope before proceeding.

For Hranna, who was missing a leg and whose sled was laden with browen meat, the bottom of that slope might just as well have been on the other side of the ocean. She saw no way to get down by herself. Hranna checked over her shoulder and sighed, thinking it might be time to test Inae's professed undying love and admiration for her. Hranna hated to admit it, but if she was going to make it to Rolly's camp, she was going to need help. Maybe she shouldn't have dumped a bowl full of flaming luftall oil into Inae's lap, thought Hranna; it was the sort of thing that might make a man uncooperative.

***

Hranna slouched with her forearms on her sled. It was dangerous to rest on the ice. But sometimes she just needed to take in the scenery. The ice floes led off into a haze of blue in the distance that could only be the ocean.

Hranna's face tingled as feeling returned to the surface of her skin. Hranna knew pain was not far away. There was nothing for it but to wait.

Bin and Moon were out of their harnesses, nuzzling the snow, looking for food. It would have been an idyllic scene were it not for the sled bearing down on her.

Hranna sensed Inae's approach. She heard his skisen snort jealously at the sight of her pair greedily gobbling up mouthfuls of buried roots.

Inae suddenly stood next to her, staring with her down onto the bed of ice floes that had once been a river. Hranna hadn't heard him approach. At least he had that going for him.

Inae was a shade taller than Hranna. His angular shoulders had yet to be rounded by hard work on the ice. In the shape of his nose and mouth, he looked a little bit like her mother, or as near like as Hranna could remember nearly nine years after her death. Hranna wished again that she'd had Rolly's talent at drawing. What wouldn't she give for a small sketch of her mother like the one Rolly had made of Hranna, that was, even now, tucked carefully away in her front pouch.

Inae broke the silence. "You going to come back with me now?"

"You going to unhitch your bucks?"

"You going to pull another stupid trick?"

"Only a frostling would have fallen for them." It was a semblance of the witty banter of their youth, but only a semblance. Things between them had changed in an instant on the ice. Even so, Hranna's upper lip and eyebrows bent upwards, acknowledging the fairness of his question. After all, in the past day she had thrown browen piss at his skisen, causing him to crash his sled, and she'd caught him on fire. He was smart not to trust her.

Inae's countenance fell. He continued to stare onto the ice floe, refusing to look at her. She'd wounded his pride. Hranna followed up quickly, "I need your help."

Inae shook his head causing his hand-me-down hood, which was much too big, to flap against his skull like a wounded bird. Hranna almost smiled, but she could tell he was in no humor for it.

"You almost killed me twice, led me on this chase, and now you want help?"

Hranna didn't respond. Sometimes a male, whether a skisen or a man, just needed to let some steam off his lungs. She looked out over the ice.

"Help with what?" he finally asked.

"I need help getting down that hill," Hranna pointed, "and a head start."

"Ha!" Inae barked out a laugh. "I'm supposed to be taking you back."

"Why?"

"I don't know. Mother sent me."

Hranna considered her next words carefully. "Anarra's dead, Inae."

Inae looked at her directly for the first time. The corners of his eyes registered a lack of comprehension.

"I killed him."

"You couldn't have." He stated it as though he was saying snow was white.

"One of my stupid tricks."

Inae's chest rose and fell. It was the only thing that moved.

"They were going to kill me," said Hranna.

"They were taking you home."

"To Inoah, who wants me dead."

"That's not—"

"Dead enough to send me injured and tired back onto the ice to bring him the blue man's treasure."

Inae didn't respond, which was fair enough.

"Inoah thinks I hid it."

"Did you?"

"Yes." Hranna pulled back the sides of her tent, revealing the blue backpack with the wealth of metal hanging from every corner.

Inae's mouth fell open. He began to speak but stopped himself. Instead, Inae shifted his weight from foot to foot, fighting off the cold.

Well, at least he had some sense, thought Hranna. Following his example, she hopped around the sled, examining the straps that held the browen meat. She realized that Inae might simply be too young to grasp the implications. She would have to lay it out for him plainly.

"Inoah—"

"I get it," he said.

"You do?"

Inae's raised eyebrows said it all: What? Did you think I was stupid? He didn't have to say it out loud, just as, apparently, she didn't have to draw him a picture of the way things stood with Inoah.

"Mother!" Inae almost spat.

It was Hranna's turn to give him a questioning look.

Inae raised his hands in a way that said, what do you think?

In a flash of intuition and insight, honed over years of village life and being a woman, Hranna grasped the situation immediately. Gyurtuh must have known about her son's crush on Hranna. She had sent him out on purpose because he was the one most likely to give her the help she needed, however crazy it might be. Gyurtuh expected Hranna to take advantage of his feelings. Could she? Not in good conscience.

"Inae—"

"I know how you feel." He walked over to unhitch his skisen. "You didn't stab me when I told you how I felt, but you did set me on fire. That's not in any of the love songs I've ever heard."

Yeah, that was true. So, Inae intended to help her regardless of her lack of feelings for him. Gyurtuh had been right after all. She had helped Hranna, despite the fact that Inoah was engaged to Hrite. Hranna never guessed that her aunt might like her as much as one of her own girls.

A speck on the horizon caused her smile to turn.

"Inae, did anyone else ride out from the village?"

"No, why?"

Hranna nodded toward the caps of the glaciers that had receded into the distance. Inae looked. He saw the figure on the sled.

Hranna whistled for her skisen. "Amrak's coming."

She didn't need to say more. Like everything else, the rest was implied.

***

"There's no time to port our sleds down the cliff. You got any tricks left?"

Inae had lashed his skisen to his sled and had pulled up alongside Hranna. Though missing a leg and injured, she'd had to wait on him—another sign of the frostling's inexperience. Well, there was no time like the present to learn.

"No tricks. Just skill." Hranna gave a conspiratorial smile.

"Not one in a hundred could make it to the bottom!"

"That's better odds than I've had this past ten-day." Hranna pulled up the edge on the blanket covering her lap. Inae's eyes grew wide. "I'm not giving you a show, pervert." Around her thighs ran the sinew cord that she carried on the sled. It looped over her legs several times, passing under the seat Balras had provided. "I might make it. But I'm thinking you? Not so much. Hyop! Hyop!"

Bin and Moon obeyed her order: Bin because she trusted Hranna; Moon because she probably couldn't see the danger they were about to get into. Hranna's sled plunged down the slope.

She hung onto the front rail. The curved hunting horn bounded around. She wished she'd tied it down tighter. Its point threatened to take out an eye.

The skisen slowed to catch their footing. Her sled bumped them in their soft rears, sending them sprinting again down the cliff to avoid being run over by the sled. They all three barreled down the steep slope.

With each jolt of the sled, Hranna slid in the seat. Thank the ocean she'd thought to lash herself to the stool.

The icy wind whipped through her hair and penetrated the thick lining of her fur jacket. Hranna shivered both at the cold and at the thrill of the mad ride.

As they reached the place where the river had frozen itself to the side of the cliff, Hranna braced for impact. Hranna saw through clenched eyes that the angle wasn't gentle enough to accept the sled smoothly. The front runners would hit first, and the rest of the sled would follow or it wouldn't.

They hit bottom. The sled shuddered. The wooden seat punched Hranna's tailbone. A jolt of pain ran up her back.

The sled tilted. It slid on one runner. Hranna leaned hard to the other side, hoping to keep it from overturning. The sled slammed safely back onto the other runner. Yet Hranna felt herself falling. Her momentum in trying to balance the sled had caused her to fall.

Hranna hit the snow face first, blocking the brunt of the blow with her hands. At least the numbness from the frostbite meant her face didn't feel the impact as much.

Pain seared through her injured arm. Hranna tumbled over and over across the ice before coming to a stop, on her back, in the snow. She couldn't move her legs. Hranna thought back to the shock she'd taken on hitting the bottom. Had she broken her back? To lose a foot was bad but to lose both legs? Hranna looked.

She nearly laughed. Her thighs were still lashed to the stool. The seat must have come loose from the sled when they hit the ice. Hranna pulled out her knife and cut the cord. It was a waste of a good rope, but time was of the essence. She couldn't lay there in the snow. She would get wet and freeze as surely as the river beneath her.

Hranna rolled away from the stool and rose carefully to her knees, testing out each muscle before trusting her weight to it. Feeling no injuries, she stood up.

Hranna missed her crutch, which was still tied to the sled.

Bin and Moon had come to a stop a little ways off. They were looking around as if someone owed them an explanation.

Hranna's head snapped to the side, eyes following as a sled bolted past her.

It was Inae, flying across the ice, whooping at the top of his lungs as he slowed to a stop near Bin and Moon.

Now Hranna smiled. One in a hundred, Inae had said. More like two in a hundred, she thought.

Maybe Amrak wouldn't be so lucky. She could hope, but he was a good hunter. If a cripple and a rider as new as fresh powder could make it to the bottom, so could Amrak. The only question is whether he would risk it. Hranna remembered the gasping last breaths of his brother, Anarra. She guessed Amrak wouldn't even pause at the top.

He was coming for them with a good team. She had two females, and Inae had a bent sled. Their only hope was to reach Rolly's people before Amrak caught them. Neither Hranna nor Inae could take the man in a fight. It was time to run.

Hranna whistled for Bin and Moon even as she searched the landscape for the last clue to the mystery of Rolly's camp. She saw it: a small black rock rising out of the icy surface of the river. Hranna set the broken seat back into the sled.

She couldn't immediately figure out how Balras had connected the stool to the sled, but he was a master with wood. She would simply have to rely on balance and hope that they hadn't far to go.

Hranna started toward the rock. Rather than cut a new path, Inae fell in behind her. Hranna took a drink from her remaining luftall oil. She wiped the back of her mitten across her face and settled in for the final leg of the chase. To someone with only one good leg left, it was the part that mattered most.

Chapter 13

The rock was farther away than it appeared. Amrak was closer than she liked. Hranna ran the calculations in her head. Inae's team was struggling to keep pace. The runners on his sled were bent inwards, channeling snow into the path of the sled. To his skisen, it must feel like they were constantly pulling uphill.

Her skisen, Bin and Moon, were slowing, despite her commands. What she wouldn't give for a little bit of browen piss. It was a thought Hranna never thought she'd have.

Hranna looked back. Amrak was closing with them. He would reach Inae first. Hranna wasn't sure what the old hunter made of their alliance. Perhaps he thought Inae was still chasing her. If he fought Inae, she might be able to reach the black rock ahead of him. She might convince Rolly's people to protect her.

Inae was practically leaning over the front of his sled, urging his skisen on with all his weight. She couldn't see his face under the hood that flapped so comically. She couldn't let him fight Amrak alone. Gyurtuh had sent Inae to help her, not to be sacrificed so that Hranna could save her own skin. And how could she ever look her friend Hrite in the eyes, having caused the death of her brother?

They would have to stand and face Amrak together, a frostling and a cripple. She saw no other way. Hranna returned her attention to the ice in front of her.

Moon's head shot up. Her tail lashed the air.

Yes, we are in trouble, little girl, thought Hranna. Bin's head remained down, pumping as she pulled the sled with all her might. Hranna looked instinctively around the ice. Something was bothering Moon, but not Bin. Maybe the inexperienced skisen, a frostling in her own right, was picking up on Hranna's mounting anxiety.

As a hunter, she didn't panic. In the midst of the crisis she felt the most aware, most alive. Her concern was for matters she couldn't directly control—what would happen to Inae now or to Rolly back in the village.

Moon continued to look up. She was causing the sled to slow even further.

"Hyop!" Hranna called out to her. "Hyop!"

Hranna saw no threat. They were on the open ice. The only object taller than the horizon was the black rock that refused to grow nearer no matter how fast they ran. There was nowhere for a pack of wollen or for a browen to hide. For them, the open ice made poor hunting grounds. For Hranna and her village, it was perfect. Especially out here, the ice on the floe might grow thin enough to spear a luftall.

Hranna's hand slid over the curved horn hafted to the pole that she used to hunt the fat, brown beasts. She examined the ice below the sled. She could tell in her gut that the ice was thinning. Hranna searched the water beneath the ice for the sign of luftall. Typical of a hunter, she thought, to be thinking about a hunt when she should be thinking of anything but.

A shadow passed under the ice in front of the sled. Luftall, she thought. It was certainly big enough. Her sled chased the shadow. They were both heading toward the black rock.

It was too big. Hranna stared at the shadow. She bent over the sled, a move that would normally have sent the skisen speeding forward. That was one nice thing about the seat Balras constructed. Hranna could give her attention to other things while she was driven across the wastes. Hranna struggled to interpret the shadow. If not a luftall, then what?

The shadow disappeared as the beast, whatever it was, sought deeper water.

Moon jerked to the left. Bin struggled against her. Hranna called out to steady the team. Moon was in a full-on panic. Hranna cursed the day she decided to brave the ice with an inexperienced skisen. Though Bin pulled straight, Moon's wild struggle against the harness caused the sled to veer left, out of line with the black rock.

Hranna shouted at Moon.

Her voice was drowned out by an enormous crash as the ice in front of the sled exploded. Moon and Bin and possibly even Hranna screamed as a figure of legend smashed into the air.

A hrall's gaping, toothy mouth opened like a fetid cave in the spot where they would have been but for Moon's frantic gyrations. Its pale, blue skin rippled with muscles as it undulated on the ice, twisting to try to get its jaws on them.

Bin suddenly gave way to Moon, deciding to trust the half-blind skisen. The sled steered wide of the creature.

Hranna stared into a lidless black eye that reflected her face back, bent and distorted. They didn't even get half-way around its massive body before the hrall's tremendous weight broke the ice beneath it, sending it back into the ocean below. Hranna watched as the shadow disappeared. She looked at the expanse of ice between her sled and the black rock. She wondered whether they would make it.

Hranna struggled to get her skisen turned back toward the rock. The hrall was hunting them. There were tales about a hrall taking a browen on the ice, dragging the clawed beast into the ocean as if it was a rabbit.

She had never even seen a hrall before except from afar, out in the ocean. The stories didn't do it justice. Its teeth were at least twice as long. Though in at least one point the tales were right. Its body really did look like a concentrated mass of malevolent souls damned to swim the ocean locked together in eternal hatred.

Looking back, Hranna saw that Inae managed to avoid the gaping hole in the ice. He was following her. He waved a rigid fist into the air. She understood his consternation. What had they done to deserve this? Hranna added a few profanities of her own.

She also noted that Amrak had not left off the chase. A sensible person would've abandoned them to their fate on the ice. Amrak must have been pushed past the point of good sense by the death of his brother.

Moon skittered again. Bin went with her. Hranna didn't even try to stop them. She didn't know how the young skisen had sensed the hrall earlier. Balras said Moon was clever. She didn't think that was what he'd meant.

Remembering Balras, Hranna leaned forward to squirt some luftall oil into the runners. The sled shot forward, not a moment too soon. A wall of blue flesh and teeth busted through the ice behind them. Breaking ice hit the back of her sled. She was leaning already. The impact tilted her dangerously forward. Hranna grabbed the front rails. The bench beneath her rose up before slamming back down as the runners reconnected with the ice.

The bench rattled off the sled taking Hranna with it. Hranna rolled to a stop. Her skisen kept running.

On her knees, with a hand on the ice, Hranna looked up at the hrall towering above her. She felt the rumble of the ice as the animal fell back into the river below.

Inae's sled raced by. She caught the briefest vision of a pair of raised eyebrows as Inae disappeared past her. She heard him holler at his skisen to stop.

"Go!" she shouted, waving him on.

He was already off his sled, running toward her. Given the timing between the previous two attacks, he'd never make it before the hrall struck again. She watched helplessly as Inae fell forward. The ice broke. His rig, with the skisen still attached, disappeared in a spray of ice and teeth. Bits of wood rained down as the hrall mangled the sled. Miraculously the skisen fell to the ice as the hrall bit through their harnesses. Their legs were pumping before they even hit the ground.

Inae pushed himself up and scrambled toward Hranna. She hadn't bothered to try standing on the ice. How was she supposed to run with only one leg?

Inae scooped his arm under her shoulder. They hobbled together away from the watery holes left by the hrall.

Hranna heard a clatter of hooves on the ice. She looked back. Inae continued struggling forward. Amrak was bearing down on them with his curved hunting horn held high. He intended to bludgeon or to impale them. She threw her weight toward the ice, taking Inae with her.

Hranna took a glancing blow off the back of her head as Amrak passed. He had missed with the point of the horn. One of the curves must have caught her, she thought, as they crumpled to the ice. If Amrak had the good sense to get off the sled, they would have already been dead. Instead, Hranna watched as he turned his skisen in a loop heading toward them again.

Hranna felt for her knife. She didn't intend to die without a fight. Before she could unsheathe it, the ground exploded in front of them.

Amrak's body broke apart like a shattered icicle as a spate of sharp teeth tore through him. He and his skisen, his entire sled, everything but a severed arm, fell into the gaping maw of the hrall.

The great beast landed on its belly on the ice. Bits of the sled and of skisen fur fell off its teeth. It stared at Inae and Hranna who lay supine on the snow. Hranna didn't dare breathe.

Then the huge beast fell through the ice. Its shadow passed under them, disappearing as the creature sought the depths of the river below.

Hranna and Inae waited for its return.

Chapter 14

"That's interesting."

Hranna didn't recognize the voice. It was a female. The accent was strange but pleasant, like talking to a villager from the north who had just come with fresh goods to trade. Hranna's eyes were closed. She might be dreaming.

"What's interesting?" said Hranna. It seemed like the right thing to say. She felt as though the conversation had already been going on a long time. That was the way with dreams.

"Your feelings are so strong for the village, but not for anyone who actually lives there."

Hranna thought about the statement. Her head swam. Was she now in the ocean, soon to be reunited with her mother? She didn't feel wet. But does a fish feel wet? Taking courage, Hranna opened her eyes.

She was in a much stranger place than the ocean. She was in a room of some kind, not rounded or made of skins. The gray walls were metal from floor to ceiling. She must be in heaven.

She'd expected more.

Hranna lay on a strange bed. The skins were white as snow, yet comfortable and remarkably thin. She could pinch them between her fingers. The room was warm but she saw no fire. Beneath the sheets, Hranna was naked. She pulled the sheets tight around her neck.

Beside her sat a young woman as white as Rolly and wearing a matching blue coat. Her hood was pulled back revealing a long fall of reddish-brown hair. She was not the woman from Rolly's book, though it could easily have been her sister. The sparkle in the woman's eyes reminded Hranna of her Aunt Gyurtuh.

"Who are you?" said Hranna.

"A woman," she said. "From far away." Hranna had heard those words before, but where. "As I said, my name is Amy."

That name sounded vaguely familiar. She tried to think, but her head felt like it was stuffed with skisen fur.

"I gave you medicine to help you sleep. Sometimes it makes people talk."

"About what?"

"Whatever."

"What did I talk about?"

"Hunting, mostly. And about a bearded young man we both know."

"Hrolly."

Amy's mouth turned up at the side as though a private joke had just passed between them. "Yes, Rolly."

Hranna's head began to clear at the mention of his name. She began to remember. Sitting up, she threw her legs over the side of the bed. Her own people slept on furs on the ground. She was surprised to see metal underneath her feet and so much space between the bed and the floor.

Looking around the room, Hranna recognized certain pieces of furniture, like the small table by the bed or the stool that Amy sat on. Yet these were unmistakably foreign. The stool had a high back that rose allowing Amy to recline against it. The table was so finely built as to make Hranna believe it had been sprung wholly made from the builder's mind. She'd thought Balras's work beautiful. She wondered what the old bachelor would make of these pieces.

"Where am I?"

"Don't you remember?"

"A little."

"You rode into our camp with Inae. Your leg and arm were badly injured. Your head was hurt and your nose nearly frozen off. Do you remember any of this? It's important that you try to remember."

Hranna forced her brain to work. It was a lot like getting a sled going on a cold morning. Slowly she began to recall what had passed on the ice.

She and Inae had given themselves up for dead. Yet the hrall hadn't returned. It must have been satisfied with Amrak. They had limped toward the rock on one sled with Inae and his skisen walking beside them. Inae's sled had been truly ruined this time.

On reaching the black rock, they found that it wasn't a rock at all, but the prow of a huge ship sticking out of the ice. High on board the ship were other blue-clad figures like Rolly. They had seen what had happened on the ice and offered to help the two hunters.

Inae tried to explain about Rolly, but it had been difficult to communicate with the men on board.

"You're lucky I came along this trip," said Amy, interrupting Hranna's thoughts. "Rolly and I might be the only two people on the planet who can speak your language. Remarkable how close Yunaut is to Kamau."

"I remember now."

"Good. Just relax." Amy's voice was so soothing. Hranna remembered the time Rolly had mentioned Dr. Amy Martin and how Hranna had resolved never to talk to the woman. How wrong she'd been.

Amy continued, "We found Rolly's journal. He wrote a lot about you."

Hranna patted her belly frantically, realizing again that she was naked. The medicine had made her forget, made her sleepy. They had taken her things, the book, the moondial, the picture Rolly had drawn of her.

"Where—"

"We took your clothes to wash. We will return them, as well as the journal and other items. Like Rolly's moondial," said Amy. "I'm a little jealous. He never even let me touch it."

Hranna didn't know how to explain that she'd taken it without his permission. Would Amy understand?

Amy continued, "He speaks of your brave fight with the beast on the ice." She leaned forward in a confidential air, "He hasn't drawn another woman since—" Amy trailed off. Hranna thought of the beautiful face staring back at her from the journal.

"Who is she?"

"The Queen," said Amy. "She's like . . . She's the wife of a great chief."

"If she's married, then why would Hrolly want her?"

Amy's eyebrow went up wryly. "She wasn't always married. That was the problem. When she got married to another man, Rolly came here."

Hranna's face blushed. Maybe consignment to the wastes was their equivalent of a woman's right to choose death for an unwelcome suitor.

Amy looked down at her white hands, crossed in her lap. She spoke quietly. "You aren't the first woman to fall for Rolly's charms." Then, cheering and smiling, she quickly added, "Don't worry. I'm the only one who speaks your language. I can keep a secret. I've kept plenty of Rolly's after all."

Hranna wondered what Amy's sad look had meant or what secrets Rolly might have entrusted to her. The thought made Hranna a little jealous.

Also, Hranna felt like her privacy had been invaded by the woman. On the other hand, the intrusion was almost welcome. Hranna hadn't shared her thoughts with anyone for so long. And because Amy was an outsider, Hranna didn't feel the usual sense of shame that she might in speaking to one of the villagers.

Amy rose to go. "I'll go see about your clothes. Don't go anywhere, Rianna."

"Hranna," she corrected the woman. "And besides, where would I go like this?" Hranna pulled at the sheets.

"Good point." Amy smiled. "Get some rest. We'll talk more in the morning." Amy tried again, "Rranna."

Close enough. Hranna gave a short nod. Amy left with a look of accomplishment on her face.

The room was different after Amy left, as if some vital spirit had been sucked out of the air. Though they had spoken only for a moment, at least to Hranna's recollection, she actually missed the strange woman.

Hranna had no idea when morning would come. Through a small circular hole in the wall, she could see the ever-blue sky. Hranna wondered that it was not freezing in the little room. Then she remembered the clear piece of ice that blocked access to the face of the moondial. It could be something like that in the hole in the wall, only bigger. She could walk across the room and see for herself. Or hop, considering that she had only one foot. Hranna looked around the room for her crutch. Not seeing it, she decided against getting out of bed.

Besides, she was tired. The bed was comfortable, despite its lack of furs. For once in the last ten-day, Hranna wasn't worried about something or someone actively trying to kill her. Anarra and Amrak were dead. Inoah would receive no report from them.

Hranna had gained some time to plan and possibly even some allies. She would explain the situation to Amy. Perhaps Rolly's party would agree to help. She'd established some room to breathe. She intended to use some of those breaths snoring.

***

Hranna examined her fur clothing as she waited for the others to arrange themselves around the table. Plates heaped with browen meat were slapped down onto the table's hard surface as each member of the team took a seat. Hranna was having difficulty adjusting to the ready presence of metal.

She'd decided soon after waking that Rolly had made a very good bargain indeed. Hranna had risked her life and lost her leg for something she thought rare beyond worth. For them, metal seemed as common as snow. Of course, for Rolly, he was bargaining on the lives of his team. She was glad they had not died.

Over the past few days, she had gotten to know Amy and was nearly as friendly with her as she had been with Hrite.

Hranna and Amy spoke at length during the latter's regular visits to Hranna's room (which was actually Amy's room, given over to her as a guest). Amy had never quite learned to pronounce her name. No matter.

Amy bunked with another female member of the team. Inae had been staying in Rolly's room, till earlier that morning.

While she waited for the group to assemble around the table, Hranna examined her furs. She appreciated how thoroughly the furs had been cleaned. They felt almost like new and smelled as bright as a new-cut tree. Hranna had discovered where Rolly got his scent. It reminded her mightily of him, sending strange waves of curiosity and guilt into her stomach.

The seven remaining teammates milled around the large room, painted the same dull gray as her sleeping quarters but appointed with decorations—drawings of wondrous, fantastical lands of green hills and tall trees.

As soon as the table was full, Hranna started to speak. Amy sitting beside her, caught her hand, giving it a pat, telling her by the gesture to wait. Hranna sat silently as the team performed their ritual obeisance to their gods.

Amy explained that the strangers didn't pray to spirits in the ocean. In fact, Amy had been fascinated by Hranna's religion, asking Hranna to tell her everything about death and the afterlife. To Hranna, it seemed almost like trying to tell a child how to walk. The questions Amy asked were so difficult that they could only have come from a child or from someone very wise. Hranna lacked the ability to answer most. When this happened, Amy kindly changed the subject, exploring another aspect of village life.

Hranna thought her village mundane and hardly worth speaking about. She'd expected to talk herself dry on the subject in a day. Yet, under Amy's active questioning, Hranna found she could not exhaust her supply of information or stories. Through Amy's eyes, Hranna saw the village expand into something nearly as infinite as the snow that it rested on.

For instance, Amy had found it endlessly amusing that the women of her village could so violently resist unwelcome advances.

Hranna's attention returned to the present as the team finished intoning and began to eat. If Amy could be believed, they prayed to a god in the sky. Perhaps they thought their ancestors floated like clouds across the face of the sun. It was a beautiful image and one Hranna could almost get behind, especially since it didn't invoke a deep-seated fear of drowning.

"Will Inae be joining us?" Amy was looking at the deserted stool where Inae had taken his meals with the team.

The young man had been fascinated by the people on the boat and how they did not build a camp but lived aboard the great metal shell.

The sides of the boat were too high for a browen to climb and the boat itself too big for a hrall to swallow. Hranna thought them as safe on board as anywhere on the ice. She felt, in fact, like a luftall on its secure cliff, which worried her, since she'd just killed a luftall who'd been too lazy.

Hranna too had grown soft in just a few days of living among Rolly's people. She needed to stay hard as ice.

"I sent Inae away."

"Where?"

She couldn't lie; not to Amy. Or she could, but simply had no desire to. Her fate hung in the balance of the next conversation. Besides, as her father said, it was better to be truthful whenever possible as a lie might be found out.

"I gave him my sled and sent him back to our village."

Amy's eyes narrowed. Hranna had seen a similar look on Rolly's face when he was thinking hard.

Hranna explained, "We need to know what's happening."

"You sent him to spy."

"To what?" The word was unfamiliar.

"Never mind."

Hranna wondered if Amy suspected her of having ulterior motives in sending Inae away. In fact, she did want information about the village and about Rolly. And she did not want Inae to be part of their plans. That way, if the plans failed, he wouldn't be blamed.

Amy spoke to the table, then, dropping into a lower voice, translated for Hranna. "I said that you have recovered and now wish to speak with us."

Hranna looked around the table, making eye contact with each of the occupants. Well, most of them anyway. A big man on her far right, named Toole, continued to shovel food into his face, seemingly un-interested in what she was about to say.

At least Toole was easy for Hranna to read, as was her new friend Amy. The rest of the group sat staring at her politely.

Used to a lifetime of interaction with people she knew intimately, Hranna found her tongue stuck to the roof of her mouth. She wished she'd had more time to get to know them before making her case.

Besides Toole and Amy, who was their healer, the other five members of the team were as different from one another as they were from Hranna. Besides the blue clothes that they wore, Hranna would be hard pressed to say how exactly they were a group. Yet, they acted like any people who have been long to-gether under hardship, like the way they'd collected their food and assembled at the table with a modicum of words and without so much as bumping elbows.

Tomas, one of the men, regarded her with watery eyes, obviously eager to return to his fare. Short and round as a luftall, Tomas was a bit of a surprise for a group that, according to Rolly, had been starving. Amy had tried to explain what each of the team mem-bers did, but their special functions eluded Hranna's limited comprehension. She simply thought of Tomas as the cook, since that was what he did, probably to be all the more close to the food supply, thought Hranna. Had Strau, the keeper of their village stores, grown so fat, there would have been a real problem. Hranna now realized that the man's unnatural skinniness was the best testimony to his fair dealing. Perhaps her father had even appointed him for that very reason.

Next to the portly Tomas sat Horkin, a man whose face and hands, in direct contrast with the rest, was as black as a browen's chest. Hranna suspected that if dropped naked onto the ice floe, his skin would melt through the surface. It was a childish thought, yet how could the white snow hope to hold such darkness? She was unable to read his eyes at all. His face was a mask, showing neither anticipation or perturbation at the pending speech. Beneath his eyes ran a mass of scars. Perhaps he could neither smile nor frown, she thought, his face having been marred by some wild creature.

The other three inhabitants of the boat were less striking. Jerome with his white beard seemingly out of place beneath a pair of keen, young eyes. Cynthia whose pale blonde hair seemed as cool as the frigid look in her eyes. And Neko, whose tan skin marked him the most similar to Hranna but whose stilted manners made him the least friendly.

Even if she had additional time to get to know the crew before making her plea, Hranna would have had difficulty anyway, given that, of the seven gathered around the table, only Amy spoke her language.

Hranna cleared her throat. In her heart, she called to the spirits of the ocean. Since Amy was translating, she would have to keep the story short, stick to the most important points. Remembering the best, most eloquent moments in her father's career, Hranna took a deep breath. Her fate rested on their reaction to what she said next.

***

"Your friend, Rolly, was injured on the ice. We met roughly six days ago. He asked for my help. We hunted together."

Amy touched her hand. Hranna waited while the woman translated. Some of the team nodded their heads. They must have gathered as much already from reading Rolly's journal. Hranna wished she could read the scratches. She wondered what he'd said about her.

As Amy's voice died away, Hranna took back up her story. "What Rolly's book may not tell you is that we were attacked by a browen, a beast that hunts on the ice. Rolly was injured. I took him to my village."

Amy translated. As Hranna listened to the strange tones coming from her friend's throat, she wondered how best to proceed. Would the truth motivate them to aid her? What might the consequences be of telling a lie? She had no time to decide. Amy had finished. Grave looks waited in anticipation of Hranna's next words, even though she knew that they must have picked up some details from Inae and from her conversation with Amy. Hranna had no idea what she'd said while under the influence of their medication.

"Rolly was still unconscious when I left him to seek your help. My father is chief of the village, but he is very old and weak." It pained her to tell the truth so bluntly when her people's entire way of communicating was based on subtlety and indirect speech. She let

Amy translate the statement and took the short break to compose herself.

"The man who will take over as chief, who already runs the village, wants Rolly dead. I do not know how long my father can prevent it or if he would rouse himself to do so."

Hranna waited before continuing, the moment had come, as important as when she faced the luftall on the open ice, as pivotal as the seconds right before Nar's horn hooked the browen's rib, as tentative as the ice under Amrak's sled before the hrall broke through.

"I need your help," she said, as simply as Rolly had said it to her. At the moment he'd said it, she'd discovered there to be a sort of magic in those words. As though that phrase opened the hearts of even a close-minded person. "I need your help to save Rolly. We must go back to the village and—"

Amy touched her hand again, saying, give me time to tell them what you've said. Hranna bit at her lip, her foot moved impatiently while Amy communicated her cause to a group of people just as foreign as the words Amy spoke. She was anxious to continue where she'd left off, to not lose momentum.

Toole interrupted Amy's speech. He was staring at meat speared on his fork when he spoke. All eyes were on him. Hranna had thought that Jerome, with his white beard, was the leader of the group based on his age and his position at the table. Her intuition began to say otherwise.

Amy looked at Hranna. "He says why would your people kill Rolly when they know he has metal, which your people value above all else?"

Hranna stared at Toole. She fought the near overwhelming urge to touch her injured ear. She could not show discomfort.

"Inoah, the new leader, thinks the wastes cannot support both of our villages. He thinks killing Rolly would stop you, that you would starve. He does not know where you are nor that I brought you supplies. He may know of my absence and may have discovered that I took meat off the dead browen, though even that might be hard to tell, since we had already harvested—"

Again Amy indicated that she should please wait while she gave Hranna's answer to Toole. The whole process, even for one used to talking around a subject, was ridiculously frustrating. Not being able to understand them or to even speak a word of their language made her feel stupid in a way nothing ever had. She resolved to learn their speech, if she was around them long enough.

Toole was speaking again, and the others were nodding, coming to his side. She recognized the signs. Cynthia was as openly receptive to Toole as she was hostile to Hranna, though Hranna did not know what she could have possibly done to engender the woman's hatred. She was satisfied to note that Toole took no more notice of Cynthia's obsequious nods than he took of Hranna's own pointed stare. Tomas too was openly nodding. Jerome appeared to concede a point. Only Horkin and Neko remained unfazed and inscrutable.

Amy raised her hand to interrupt, but the man kept right on talking till finally, he deposited the bite of meat in his mouth. The crunch of his jaw was the only sound in the room.

Amy's lips puckered and her eyebrows went all squiggly in concentration, "He says—well, he said a lot, but basically he thinks your village has too many people for us to rescue Rolly and that Rolly can take care of himself and that, besides, we have enough meat now to last out the moon cycle and can use one of our own moondials to guide us to our village in the north." Amy took a breath.

Hranna broke in, "Inoah thinks I buried the treasure that Rolly used to pay for the luftall we killed. If I don't return with it, Inoah says he's going to kill Rolly."

Amy translated.

Toole shrugged. He said only one word.

"Maybe," Amy translated.

If she had two good feet, Hranna would have stood and challenged the oafish Toole to a fight. The big man could easily beat her, but she wouldn't die without taking his life with hers. She was that mad. Her hand went to the hilt of her knife.

Amy intervened. "Rranna, he thinks—" She collected her thoughts. "He thinks that Inoah, as a man, might say one thing to you and do something different. He doesn't think Inoah will kill Rolly. Toole thinks Inoah was just using you as one means of getting at Rolly's metal. Rranna, Toole hates women. He's a jerk."

Hranna didn't know the sound of that word, "jerk," but she understood the sentiment perfectly. A jerk indeed. Hranna calmed her beating heart. She remembered what her father had said about Inoah. He thought like a chief. Meaning, he thought like Hranna's own father had once thought. From experience, Hranna knew that her father could be just as ruthless. The difference was she had always understood her father's motives and secretly applauded even his most brutal actions. She considered the situation now from Inoah's point of view.

"Rranna—" Amy began.

"Toole's right."

Amy's head twitched to one side. "What?"

"He's right. Tell him that."

Amy's eyes never left Hranna as she repeated the statement in the stranger's speech. She was studying Hranna's face, which was now as unyielding a mask as the one that shadowed Horkin's black face.

"He's right. I've been a fool. He took the thing that I wanted and used it against me. He stood nothing to lose if I died and would profit from my death since I alone am a challenge to his legacy."

Amy made a move to ask her to pause, but this time Hranna insisted on speaking, still looking at Toole, who finally looked back at her. His head was tilted slightly back so that she was looking at the barest fraction of his forehead. Nevertheless she felt the weight of his full attention. He was, in his own way, as formidable as Inoah or as Rolly, especially since he lacked Rolly's social grace.

She continued. "Inoah threatened to kill Rolly if I did not return with the treasure. He sent his men out to follow me. Perhaps they meant to take me back to Inoah. Perhaps they meant to take the treasure from me and to leave my body for the snow to bury."

Amy translated. Toole gave one sharp nod. He spoke again, this time with his concentration still fixed on Hranna. He did not blink and his eyes never wavered.

Amy spoke back at him quick and sharp. Multiple voices added to hers as Cynthia and Tomas joined the conversation. Jerome came in, but in a soothing, placating sort of tone. Horkin and Neko remained silent. Toole seemed to take no notice of the heated debate. He was looking at Hranna.

He said two words. The speakers went silent.

"He said," Amy began.

"Wait," said Hranna, "What did he say at the last?" Though this conversation concerned her own fate, Hranna could not help but be fascinated by the power dynamic. Besides, she didn't need to know what he said. He was obviously in charge. No one was going to go against him. If he told them to take her up to the top of the boat and throw her down onto the ice, Tomas and Cynthia would have taken her legs and

Jerome her arms, under protest of course. For Hranna, who loved to know how things worked, the final words were much more interesting than anything else that had been said that day.

"He said, 'Tell her.'" Amy reported.

Ah, Hranna thought. Here was one who knew that she would understand. He did not hate women, as Amy said. Not exactly. Toole, thought Hranna, hated everyone equally. Himself perhaps most of all, which is why he did not care about their opinion of him. What Toole cared about, as much as Hranna loved metal, was common, good sense. Like Hranna, he was, above all else, a practical man. Hranna set her jaw as Amy began to explain. Toole had made his decision. The rest would not oppose him. She did not want her face to accidentally betray her as she heard her own death sentence pronounced.

"He says that if you think taking metal back to your village will save Rolly, then you should do that. He says we will honor Rolly's bargain and more. But," Amy's face went even whiter, were that possible, and she stared down at her hands, "while he thanks you for the meat, you are also eating that meat now, and we can't afford to continue to feed you if we are to have enough to last on our journey to our village."

Hranna saw the finality of it.

"I will go."

"But you haven't a sled."

"I can manage."

Amy turned to the group and began to protest in loud, incomprehensible terms. Toole waved her off nonchalantly with his empty fork. Amy looked beseechingly at the others. Only Horkin and Neko returned her gaze, but their countenances had not changed.

In a surprising turn of events, Horkin spoke. Neko nodded.

Hranna waited to hear what the dark man had said that the other found so compelling as to break his composure.

Amy turned back to her. "We can help you with the sled. We have such things on our boat that can be modified for your needs. Horkin says he will help with the preparations and Neko as well. Oh, Rranna, I'm so sorry. If Rolly were here—"

"But he isn't," said Hranna. "What Toole suggests makes sense. Please tell him I said so."

"But—"

"Please."

"Oh, all right." Amy communicated the message, though Hranna suspected that Amy added a few of her own choice words into the mix. It didn't matter. Toole got the point. He nodded twice and turned back to his food. The others did likewise. Only Amy was not eating.

Hranna took up her own fork, a metal instrument she'd recently mastered. She took a bite of the browen meat and looked at Amy as if to say, look, I can eat, so should you. Amy refused to budge.

"It's okay, Amy."

"It's not okay."

"What is my survival to these people? I am a dangerous inconvenience to them." As she was in her own village too, she was thinking.

A knot formed in the pit of her stomach, yet she continued to eat. On a hunt, you ate and slept whenever you could. Plus the food was not bad, although the spices were as strange to her as the surroundings. She had to admit that Tomas was a good cook.

She had killed Anarra. True, it was an accident and might not be discovered. Amrak too was dead. Hopefully Inae had the good sense to make up a convincing story.

It didn't matter. Hranna was being sent back onto the ice, with a sled full of rich metal, yes. But Inoah already told her how fleeting riches could be if you lacked the means to protect them. He would take them from her and kill her, not tell Rolly, and then bargain afresh with the stranger should he ever awake. It was what her father would have done, aside from killing her, if he was still in charge of the village, which he most certainly was not.

She could offer to help the team get to their village. Yet they would not need her once the moon rose. Had the moon not hidden its face, she would never have met Rolly.

She could take her wealth and go on her own way, maybe trade with another village for the provisions she'd need to survive on the ice. But why wouldn't that village just kill her and take what she had? Maybe if she parceled it out?

No. They would track her the same way Inoah had. One day, her luck would give out. The bad luck demon following her would see to that.

And besides, you couldn't eat metal. You couldn't talk to metal or laugh with it. Looking around at the drab gray walls of the boat, she could see what metal was really worth.

Hranna resolved to return to the village. They were her people. If the villagers thought she should die and were willing to stand by while Inoah killed her, then perhaps they were right.

Toole rose from the table and was followed out of the room by Horkin and Neko. Hranna slipped out a short time later to prepare for her final journey across the ice.

Chapter 15

Hranna needed a walk. Normally, a hike on the trails around the village would cool off her head. Here in the boat, the air remained uniformly warm no matter where she went, even though she never saw a fire. Also, back home, she'd never had to contend with a crutch. The resounding clank from the wooden stump as it hit the metal floor made the fit she was throwing more satisfying but also more clumsy.

Hranna could travel through the vessel without wearing gloves or her outer furs. She continued to wear them out of habit and because the rest of the crew wore the same blue clothing that Rolly had worn on the ice. Hranna hadn't stopped to consider that their clothing might be more forgiving to changes in temperature than her own.

Indeed there were times on board ship when Hranna felt positively warm, a condition that, in her village, only happened when you took a long pull from a flagon of luftall oil or shared a blanket with several cousins. The sensation was almost uncomfortable to one whose skin had grown used to the wintry climes of the wastes.

It had been a disastrous meal. Hranna ran over the conversation in her mind, looking for any way she might have turned the tide in her favor. She recalled every word, at least of the ones she understood, and every gesture.

Hranna did not dwell on the loss in a moribund way. And if she'd been asked to recount the event to Gyurtuh, she would not have recreated the scene to garner sympathy. Many a village girl had tried this approach with Hranna before finding her observations and solutions to their obvious problems too practical. They hadn't wanted an answer, they'd just wanted to vent. Hranna had never understood that. She wanted to understand.

The halls of the ship were just as good a place as an ice trail for dwelling on unfortunate events. She wandered the length of them. Hranna had been given no instructions to remain in or out of certain areas. If not in actual size, the layers of rooms stacked on top of one another made the boat even larger than her village.

She knew from the tour Amy had given her when she was well enough to walk, that Toole, Horkin, and Neko would be working in the large cavern that was below and toward the front of the vessel. When she came to that room, Hranna stood on a railing overlooking rows of wooden boxes. Horkin wrestled with a shiny, long piece of metal while Toole attacked its end with a blue fire as bright as Rolly's red star. The fire seemed to leap from his fingertips. His head was covered in a strange metal hood.

A ten-day ago she might have mistaken Toole's actions for magic. She had since seen the moondial up close as well as Rolly's star maker.

These were not magic, just clever devices like Balras might have managed to build if he had sufficient tools and ingredients. Putting her hand up against the glare of the blue flame, Hranna looked closely at Toole till she spied a thin bladder running across his arm to the floor and from the floor to a metal tube behind him. Hranna reasoned that the flame must be spitting from that tube in the same way smoke issued from the other end of a chimney bladder. It was a fascinating concept.

Horkin, spying her up in the gallery, gave a tight wave before returning his concentration to bending the metal. Other pieces of metal were lying about, waiting for a similar fate.

Neko, meanwhile, sat at a small table to one side, drawing on a sheet the same way Rolly had done with his journal. Hranna wondered what kind of thoughts or images he was recording. She walked around the railing till she was at an angle to see his work.

Neko was drawing a most fantastic looking sled. He'd made scratches and symbols along the length of the runners and at the curve where the runners rose to the front to cut at the ice. The design looked beautiful, and the rider had a wicked smile on her face. Hranna's head jerked back with the realization that the rider was her.

The rider, who was perched on a stool like Balras had made but a little higher, had only one foot. That could only be Hranna. Neko glanced up at Hranna and made some slight adjustment to the figure's face. Hranna's hand reached for her ear. She wondered if he'd captured that particular defect.

Based on Neko's drawing, Hranna grasped that Horkin and Toole were reshaping one of their own metal sleds to match her needs. Though she'd been devastated about being kicked out onto the ice, part of her began looking forward to chance to test Neko's design.

With a last look over her shoulder at the builders, Hranna left the large cavern. She retraced her steps toward the upper levels and her own room where she might begin packing her limited belongings.

She hadn't been entirely lazy during her brief recovery. Hranna had managed to repair the tent that had been damaged by Bin during the browen's first attack. Instead of skisen sinew, Amy had taught her how to sew using a roll of fine string. The stuff was so thin that she had to look carefully to see it. No wonder their clothing was so infinitely better than their own. There was no end to how much nicer their possessions were.

Passing by an open doorway, Hranna paused. The sight inside confirmed her thoughts. The room was lined from floor to ceiling with books. A warm yellow glow issued from the doorway like the last light of the sun on evenings when it set. Curiosity overwhelmed her better judgment.

Hranna peeked inside. Amy had her back to the doorway, her hands extending onto a polished wooden table. Hranna, whose instincts were honed from years of living elbow to elbow, knew that she'd intruded on a private moment. Where she came from, those were almost as sacred as the ocean.

She turned quietly to go. Unfortunately, the knocking of her crutch against the door frame betrayed her presence.

"Don't go," said Amy.

Hranna skulked back into the room with her shoulders hunched over the crutch. She could tell Amy had been crying, though she did not comment on it and neither did Amy, who sat back against the large table.

"They're so stupid."

"No, they aren't," said Hranna. She stumped toward her friend, wanting to look at the amazing books on the shelves but knowing her duty was to the conversation. "They made the right choice for themselves."

"Toole—"

"Was thinking like a chief," said Hranna, echoing her father's own words about Inoah. "Sometimes a chief has to make tough decisions."

"He's not our chief."

Hranna raised her eyebrows by way of challenging the statement.

"That never would have happened if Rolly was here. Rolly knows how to get at Toole."

"If Rolly was here, the result would be the same. I would be leaving having fulfilled my promise."

"Are you sure you wouldn't have stayed," said Amy, wiping the back of her thumb up the corner of her eye, which now sparked with a bit of mischief, "considering the company?"

"Rolly?"

"Stranger things have been known to happen. Alone on the ice. Facing danger. Sharing a tent."

Hranna avoided her friend's gaze, pretending to be fascinated by a beautiful gold engraving on the side of a nearby book.

"I'm hardly a queen," she said as her hand drifted toward her ear.

"Stop that." Amy caught her by the forearm, reminding Hranna of how Rolly had grabbed her on the ice when she'd tried to snatch the moondial. "Why do you do that?"

"Do what?"

Amy ignored her protestation, continuing to hold her arm and conveying her sincerity by look and by point of contact. "You're beautiful. Plus, you're the daughter of a chief. That's got to count for something, right?"

Hranna again looked around the room. "Around you, I feel like a skisen dropping on fresh snow."

Amy laughed. "Don't be ridiculous."

"All of the things you have—"

"Took us generations to achieve. In a climate much more forgiving than this." Amy put her hand on a round object on the desk beside her. It spun easily under her hand. Hranna watched as a blur of colors swept over the face of the circle.

"It's called a globe," said Amy. "And we are here."

Amy stabbed at the globe, arresting its momentum suddenly. Her finger pointed to the edge of a great expanse of white. "You call this the waste." Amy's hand moved over the white. "From where we are here," Amy pointed with the smallest tip of her pinky finger, "to our camp up north here," her finger barely moved, "is about six or seven days away. Or one day by boat if the river hadn't frozen."

Hranna's face had moved close to the globe. She examined intently the places marked by Amy. She understood the concept of a map, though her people never bothered with them, trusting to their instincts on the ice and because they preferred to remain so close to home. Usually maps were rough things drawn quickly in the snow and used to organize a hunt or a battle—though she'd never been to war, owing to her father's resourceful diplomacy.

If what Amy was saying were true, the size of the wastes overwhelmed her mind. It ran like a hood over the top of the globe.

"This globe is our world: real name Hart's Planet, but we call it Hurt."

Amy continued, "I know it's hard for you to believe; the planet is round. We didn't believe it either till our smartest and bravest people—people like Rolly—proved it." Amy spun the globe again, slowly. "He was the first to sail around the whole world, you know?"

Hranna did not know. She couldn't even appreciate what Amy was saying. Her head was spinning as much as the globe itself.

"We live down here in Danyfyr." Amy stopped the globe, pointing to a colorful stretch that ran around the middle of the globe like a wide, well worn belt. Hranna looked at the image and thought of the green paintings in the galley where they'd just eaten. Were those really to be believed as well?

"Rolly thinks we didn't always live there." Amy returned her hands to the table behind her and her eyes to Hranna's. "He thinks that we came from somewhere on the wastes, a long, long time ago."

Hranna simply shook her head.

"It gets weirder," said Amy. "Rolly doesn't think we are native to Hart's Planet. He says there are some pictures and words in the oldest books that have some animals we recognize, like rabbits, but nothing like skisen or browen." Amy sighed. "He established our camp here years ago in the hopes of exploring. He thinks the answer is somewhere in the wastes. But he never had the chance to look, at least not till now."

"Till the queen?"

"Exactly." Amy nodded, clearly glad that Hranna was following along so well and hadn't simply walked out the door at the first mention on Rolly's wild theories. Amy didn't yet appreciate, thought Hranna, that tracking a conversation came as easily to her people as tracking a luftall under the ice. Meanwhile, theological conjectures about origins felt like so much useless theology. People could believe what they wanted. It didn't bother Hranna.

"We're his team," said Amy. "We followed him around the world, picking up Horkin and Neko along the way," she rolled her eyes, "long story. I'll tell you later."

If there is a later, thought Hranna.

"And now we've followed him to the end of it."

"He's that important to you?" said Hranna.

"He's that important to the whole world."

"Then I'll do my best to get him back."

Amy took her hands in hers, obviously about to cry again. Hranna, to whom the statement was as straightforward as saying the "sky is blue," wondered if she'd ever get a chance to look at the books.

***

The straps that anchored the sled to the boat were still taut. She was eager to detach them. Eager to actually own the fantastic machine, even if it did mean leaving the boat.

Bin and Moon stamped impatiently nearby. They'd grown used to having their own way, foraging at will around the hull of the ship, though there was not much food to be had on the face of the frozen river.

She still didn't trust her eyes as they'd lowered the sled from the deck of the boat down onto the ice via a series of ropes. Hranna's mind wanted to focus on the metal gears used for the heavy lifting and the small circles of metal that bore the weight of the sleigh and all her belongings. She wondered whether Balras could make anything like them.

It had taken Toole, Horkin, and Neko the better part of the previous day to outfit the sled for her use. In that day Hranna had seen wonders.

They had a metal cylinder that breathed fire through a small bladder, fire hot enough to cut and bend metal. Amy showed her the library, a room full of books, filled with the experience and thoughts of their culture's best minds.

Given the chance, she would have lived quietly in that room, not eating, not sleeping, not consuming precious supplies. To know what those writers knew, if only for a moment, seemed better than taking her chances again on the bleak, barren landscape.

Snow blew slowly across the ice floes that coated the river. The wind carried it in shifting swirls toward the horizon, white on white as far as her eyes could see.

She stood at the center of a half-circle of blue coats. Amy had come to see her off. Toole was busy worrying over something on the sled. Horkin and Neko stood by as glum as ever. Even old Jerome had left the boat to say goodbye.

Amy patted Hranna on the shoulder. "You're going to be all right, Rranna."

Hranna's head fell to one side. She could not face the kindness.

"I have a sled, my skisen, and a horn for the hunt."

"That's not what I meant."

Hranna met Amy's gaze with a wry smile. The woman knew her story, all about her trouble with the village and with Inoah. But that trouble was not their trouble, not the blue-people's trouble, Hranna kept reminding herself. She had been wrong to ask them to intervene in the life of the village as though they were gods—as if Hranna herself were more capable of leading the village than Inoah.

When she'd been with Rolly and, later, during her few days on board their ship, she had seen how many more possibilities life held. But that kind of life did not involve a village. Rolly's people had left their own villages behind long ago—though they still yearned for them, as the green landscape in the galley showed.

Hranna did not know what fate had in store for her. Already she was Hranna the Luftall Hunter and Hranna the Browen Slayer. Hranna the finder of strange, rich men on the ice, as Gyurtuh had said. Hranna of the Silver Sled.

She did not yet know what more she might become. Her hand touched the hilt of the knife that her father had given her. It seemed crude in construct to the tools she'd seen on board ship. Yet she was proud to own it and foolish enough to hope that she might not be the last one to do so. Hranna the Mother. Would she ever own this title? Hranna bringer of life and nurse to hunters?

She was surprised that it mattered so much to her. Life on the ice had always been enough. Hranna hadn't even thought of having a family till she found that she couldn't have one.

Somber thoughts filled her mind as she hitched Moon and Bin to the silver sled. Hranna missed Nar. She hadn't even had time to mourn his loss.

Her fingers worked quickly on the cords that attached the skisen harness to the sled. For once, she could use all her fingers. Horkin had given her a pair of blue gloves, just as she'd asked Rolly, who must have recorded her request in his journal.

Horkin stepped forward. His deep voice matched the darkness of his face and the scars under his eyes. Though she could not understand his words, she caught the intent behind them.

"He says he's sorry for you to go. And sorry for your villager who perished on the ice."

"That was no great loss," said Hranna. Had Amrak lived, she would be dead.

"I know," said Amy. "Horkin feels responsible. He was in large room, praying to his gods when the big beast came."

"I'm sure he can't have caused it."

"You haven't heard how he calls out once every ten-day," said Amy. "It's loud enough to think a god might listen."

Hranna held her gloved hand out toward Horkin. "Thank you, for everything."

He cocked his head to one side, looking at her extended arm.

"They don't hold hands with a woman where he is from," said Amy.

"Oh," said Hranna. "Neither do we. I mean, we don't take hands either." She simply nodded toward the big man.

He returned the gesture.

Neko stepped forward. He presented her with a long piece of metal, twisted at one end and curiously flat on the other.

"It's a crutch, one of his own invent," Amy explained. "The curved bit goes under your arm and the bent bit touches the ground, springy like."

Putting her weight on the new crutch, Hranna felt it give underneath her. She thought the ice was falling and quickly pulled her weight back. Neko smiled. Hranna looked at the ice. It was perfectly solid.

She tried the crutch again, this time watching more closely. It bent under her weight and bore her slightly back up. It was, as Amy had said, as springy as a bent limb.

"How can I thank you all, for everything?" said Hranna.

Hranna patted the load atop the front of the sled. She had Rolly's book and his backpack too, resupplied with medicine and food packets and shiny metal objects. The moondial was stashed in its front pocket. Rolly hoped to give it to his future son. Hranna would see that he had that opportunity if it were within her power to save him.

Toole had another moondial. And besides, they all knew how fond Rolly was of the instrument. It was a fine piece, noted Neko, if not a little antiquated.

Neko had a passion for the proper measuring of objects, a study he called mathematics.

Neko said that, while he appreciated the simplicity of the moondial, he needed harder instruments for the application of his trade. He showed her great lumbering metal beasts that ate metal by the bite and stored knowledge, just like a book, on each bitten metal card.

Horkin's area of expertise had been more difficult for Amy to describe. He wanted to know the connection between things. Hranna thought she understood. Maybe it resembled her own need to know how systems worked.

Finally, she checked the second bundle: a blue pack of her own, containing enough metal to buy her ransom with some left over for a dowry if Inoah would relent and let her take a husband. He might find it difficult to refuse the request of Hranna of the Silver Sled. The villagers would resent him if he did, especially the family ambitious enough to want to marry into her wealth, and this at a time when Inoah needed to consolidate his power.

He'd said he could take whatever she had by force. Perhaps he was right. Though her arm was healing from Rolly's medicine and Amy's care, and thankfully none of Yansil's liquid bile, she still had no leg. Even fully formed, she couldn't take Inoah in a fight without the aid of tricks or of luck, which had been in such short supply for her. Thankfully, Toole had given her a metal tube with two red stars. Inoah might find himself with a face full of fire if he tried anything stupid. Hranna patted the round outline of the tube where it bulged at the side of her blue pack.

Tomas and Cynthia looked down from the side of the boat. She'd learned little about them. They'd avoided her after the vote, perhaps from a sense of guilt or out of indifference. Hranna could not tell, nor did it particularly matter.

Jerome had come to see her off. He walked to her as she mounted the sled. Toole had fashioned, under Neko's supervision, a metal hybrid between a bench and a seat so that Hranna could ride nearly standing, as she liked, without bearing her full weight on her one foot. She even thought that with some practice, she might teach Bin and Moon to respond to shifts In weight from her single foot.

Jerome raised his hand. Hranna recognized it as a sort of religious invocation of their spirits. He then placed that hand on her shoulder. It felt unnaturally heavy.

He motioned for Amy to translate.

"I pray you a blessed journey, hunter, and thank you for the food."

"Metal is thanks enough."

He shook his head sadly, as if he deeply regretted their parting, though he'd been one of the ones who voted for it. "I have two girls at home. They'd be about your age. I'm—"

Hranna understood his sentiment. He wished her to exonerate him from her death. It was no matter to her, but of great import to him.

Taking his hand off of her shoulder and shaking it as Rolly taught her to do, Hranna gave the man a knowing look and a nod. They understood each other. Or at least, she understood him and knew he would never understand her or even himself for that matter; her understanding was enough for them both. He was absolved.

Jerome stepped toward the back of the sled, waiting for her to go. Amy came alongside again, slipping Hranna a small packet covered in brown paper.

"It's a gift," said Amy, "A notebook like Rolly's. Every adventurer ought to keep a journal."

Amy indicated she should unwrap the present. Buried inside the decorative paper was a book whose pages were as white as the snow.

Hranna simply stared at it. She flipped open the front and the back, leafed through the pages and stared.

"It's not what you expected?" Amy sounded disappointed.

Hranna shut the book, looking with eyebrows curved inquisitively at her friend.

"I can't write."

"You'll figure it out," said Amy. "You just make up a symbol for each sound. See, this is the letter 'R' for Rranna." Amy traced it with a stick.

"Hranna." She laughed despite herself at the exasperated look on her friend's face.

"I thought I had it."

"Close enough."

"Well, make up the symbol for Rranna however you like. I'm sure you can do it."

Hranna thought the woman was going to hug her. Thankfully, the awkward moment passed.

Suddenly, Hranna was struck by her lack of propriety. "It is a day of wondrous gifts. Yet I have nothing to give you in return."

"You don't need to—"

"Wait."

Hranna reached into her inner pocket. It was easy to do with the warm, thin blue gloves. She removed the rolled up piece of paper that Rolly had given her. It was a little worse for the wear. Her picture was still clearly visible in the drawing.

"Take it. Remember me."

"I can't. It's yours."

"I might be buried by the snow within a day or two. I do not wish everything to be buried with me." Hranna thought of her precious knife and of the moondial.

"Enough," Hranna said, turning on Amy. "A hunter does not cry on the ice." Her friend's shoulders had started trembling in anticipation of tears. "Frozen tears may burn your face. You must be strong if you are to cross the ice to your metal village. Promise me."

"I will be," said Amy.

"Good." Hranna grinned. "See you in the sky, Amy Martin."

"Or you, in the ocean," said Amy.

Hranna called out to Bin, shifting her weight forward as she did so. It was never too early to begin training. They might sense her weight by the end of this trip. Whether she would be alive to keep training them afterward, only time would tell.

Chapter 16

From the top of the frozen riverbank, Hranna looked back over the ice at the same image Rolly had captured in his book of a black rock sticking out against a horizon of snow. She wiped a blue glove across her nose, missing the universal warmth of the foreign ship and the company too, but also feeling a gladdening in her heart to be under the open sky, her runners facing the world. Technically, she could go anywhere—technically.

During the trek across the ice, Hranna's eyes had never left Moon's tail, watching carefully for any sign of a hrall. Amrak's severed hand still waved mournfully from the ice where it had fallen. Hranna skirted the gaping holes, avoiding the larger pieces of Inae's old sled. A hrall would regret trying its teeth on her new ride.

As Toole indicated, metal was much more durable than wood. Her new sled ran well on the ice and was just as light if not lighter than the sled Balras made. The old bachelor would certainly want a look at it.

It had easily handled the drive up the riverside. Had she still been on Balras's sled, Hranna would have considered moving it to the top part by part—certainly a challenge in her present state of one-leggedness.

Hranna wondered if that was how Inae had managed. Probably the impetuous frostling had raced right up the slope, unaware of the mortal danger of a broken runner. He didn't have the best record with sleds either, thought Hranna, though most of his misfortunes in that department had been her fault.

The glacial peaks cut like teeth through the horizon in front of her. Pointing the sled to the left of the farthest peak, Hranna told Moon and Bin to move out.

She called an immediate halt.

Like pieces of gristle marring the glaciers' white smile, came a large group of sleds, moving in a wedge like a war party (and not single file as was most efficient).

Hranna didn't have to guess who was at the front point of the horn formation. Her father had ridden there once. Now it would be Inoah.

Turning her head, Hranna saw the black obelisk still standing out from the icy surface of the river. She couldn't return there. To her left lay the ice bridge and the open waste beyond it. If she made a break for it, Inoah might let her slip away. She could cut in behind them, maybe burn down Inoah's tent before she broke with the village forever. Yet that tent one day soon would belong to her best friend, Hrite.

Could she strike out in Rolly's last direction, maybe making it to their fabled village of metal ahead of them? And if she reached it, what then? Pillage it? Take as many red stars and as many precious items as her sled could carry? Even if she could find their village, it seemed like a betrayal of her new friend Amy.

Though the entire world lay before her, Hranna's path through it was narrow.

Hranna urged her skisen forward again, riding toward her fate, tall and proud, atop the silver sled.

***

The look on Inoah's face was almost as priceless as the sled on which Hranna rode. Hers was a mask.

The entire party drew to a halt as she approached. The front sleds formed a wall with Inoah at the center. The rest of the sleds grouped behind them. So it was not entirely a party of war, Hranna noted. Some sleds were being kept back in a protected stance. Still there were enough sleds facing her that, had she been a single enemy foolish enough to ride toward them, she would have been surrounded in an instant. As it was, they formed an impassible wall of skisen and wood.

Hranna's sled faced Inoah's. Yanka rode to his right.

Inoah was clad head to foot in Rolly's blue clothes.

So he had not honored their bargain, just as Toole had said.

This meeting was pointless. Hranna looked for a way to escape. Her hand reached not for her knife but toward the metal tube inside the backpack.

"It was a foolish thing you did," said Inoah.

Anger sprang instantly to her throat at the open upbraiding. How dare he speak to the daughter of the chief with such impunity, Hranna marveled. Though she seethed inside, she managed to keep her voice civil.

"And what was that?"

"Trading with the strangers." His arm extended, encompassing the riding party. "Cutting the village out of the riches."

"I merely fulfilled the promise I'd made to the blue man."

"At the cost of two good hunters."

Hranna inhaled. So, Inoah knew that Anarra and Amrak had not returned. But how did he know they were dead?

Looking past the line of sleds, Hranna's heart leaped in her chest. There in the group, behind the lead sleds, she spied a unique set of runners. She could not see the driver but was sure that, if she could, she would see a young frostling with his face obscured by an oversized hood.

Inae must have been intercepted on his way back to the village. The stupid boy must have led them back to the boat.

No, that was unkind, thought Hranna. They would have easily followed his trail. She wondered how much Inae had said.

"The ice took them," she said. It was what her people said of a hunter who did not return. Theirs was a dangerous life. Bodies were not always recovered. To be buried by the snow was an honor that even Inoah could not contradict without speaking ill of the dead. If he was going to accuse her, now was the time.

"Maybe so, but—"

Hranna inwardly breathed a sigh of relief. Inae had not blabbed. Inoah was now on guard. Hranna remembered again just how long she'd been playing this game and how easily Inoah was verbally routed. The time was right for her to strike, while he was still off balance.

"Let me pass," said Hranna.

Inoah stared at her. If his skull were a metal tube, thought Hranna, she might have been consumed by a red, flaming star.

"You will join our party."

A chill ran up Hranna's spine. As daughter of the chief, she still outranked Inoah socially and should have merited deferential treatment. Either his brazenness resulted from being so far from the village or it had a different, more sinister origin.

"I will do no such thing. I will go back to my father."

"Your father is dead," said Inoah.

Hranna put a blue-gloved hand to her mouth.

Inoah continued, reveling in having the upper hand. "He died when the Tent of Meeting burned."

Hranna gasped. "That's not possible."

"Why is that?" Inoah's look bore the same intensity of animal hatred as the black eye of the hrall. "Accidents happen, Hranna."

Yanka sneered. Had this been a real party of war, thought Hranna, the waterwan would be shivering safely in the ocean spouting visions while the rest risked their lives.

Two thoughts competed for control of her mind: Inoah had killed her father and Inoah was chief.

"I must go to him."

"What was left of his body was seen to," said Yanka. "His spirit is now in the ocean."

The implication was clear. If Hranna wanted to see her father again, they would most certainly oblige her. She eased her hand off of the metal tube. She'd only give them an excuse.

At least they were together now, she thought, her mother and her father, together in the never freezing expanse of water. Or perhaps in the sky as Amy said. Hranna looked up.

"We are on our way to trade with the strangers," said Inoah. "From the look of it we should all be rich if they give such treasures for a hunk of browen meat. Fall in behind us."

It was not a request.

Inoah leaned forward. His sled passed closely by hers. Yanka's flanked her other side.

"Soon," Inoah whispered.

The skinny waterwan cackled.

Hranna shuddered. Inoah spoke of a final reckoning. She could not buy or bargain her way out of it. She had ridden back to her death all for the sake of a man she hardly even knew and who must be as dead as her father.

***

As the lead sleds passed, the secondary group formed up. Hranna turned her sled in a tight loop, coming up among them, guiding herself toward Inae's rig.

Other friendly faces were in tow. Balras gave her his usual warm smile—though the one he gave Moon was even brighter—before examining her sled with a keen eye that, unlike Inoah's, held no envy.

Balras drove a sled even stranger than the one he'd given Hranna. For one thing, it was drawn by four skisen, not two. For another, it held more than one rider. Hranna thought she recognized the huddled form of Yansil the village healer. She struggled to understand what could possibly draw the old woman onto the ice—maybe a chance at more metal pouches?

The old woman had not fulfilled her promise to keep Rolly safe. Hranna did not blame her. She'd hardly expected the healer to stand in Inoah's way, especially if he was violent enough to do away with her father.

"Hranna!"

Another of the fur clad riders hailed her. Dressed as they all were in luftall skins, her people were often hard to tell apart, though she'd spent so much time around them that even the smallest mannerism might give them away. She didn't recognized this rider immediately. His accent certainly was strange enough. And his face...

A pair of blue eyes regarded her from beneath a hood of luftall skin. Had Hranna not been seated, she might have fallen off her sled.

Rolly was driving the sled as if he'd been born to it.

***

If Hranna could have leapt off her sled and hugged Rolly, she would have. It was as though he was back from the dead.

"I told you I'd have to sleep for a while."

"I thought—" said Hranna

"You speak?" Balras said to Rolly.

"I told you he did," said Hranna.

"Yes, but what came out of his mouth before held less sense than my skisen."

"I thought it best not to reveal how well I knew your language," said Rolly.

"It was my tea that did it." Yansil inserted herself into the conversation. "Can cure anything, even stuck tongue."

Balras had a sound reply for her, "Yet you had to come along and see that your foolproof cure took. Is that what you're saying, old woman?"

At the mention of Yansil's tea, Hranna had seen a familiar grimace pass across Rolly's face, the same as when he'd picked luftall gristle off his tongue that first day.

She gave him a knowing smile.

"Thank you, Yansil," Rolly said, rather more loudly than he had to. "I wouldn't be here if it weren't for your teas."

He dropped his voice so that only Hranna could hear. "The smell kept certain undesirables from poking around the tent."

"Look at you," she said.

"And you," said Rolly. "I see my people were nice to you."

"Nice enough to send me back to my death."

Rolly frowned. She wondered how much he understood. How much he'd been told by Inoah or the others.

"They were kind," she added, "especially Amy—"

"I knew you'd like her."

"But now that Inoah is chief—" Hranna paused. She'd never shared any of this with him. Though he'd certainly get the story from Amy, provided any of them survived the coming encounter.

Hranna continued, "I only came back because Inoah said he'd kill you if I didn't bring him your treasure."

"My what?" Rolly sounded outraged. Surely he must have suspected some of this. Had Yansil told him nothing? Then again, what did the old woman know that was worth telling? And he had apparently been faking ignorance of their language.

"He suspected that I had hid something of yours, something of value," she said, "which I did."

Hranna reached under her mended tent. Picking up the blue pack by its handle, Hranna tossed it to Rolly.

He caught it, but not without leaning, which caused his skisen to turn, almost sending his sled into hers. Hranna shook her head.

"Just like a frostling."

"A what?"

"New to the ice, like the first frost."

Now he smiled too, especially as he discovered the restored state of his pack. Hranna knew that everything was in it. She'd insisted on packing it herself.

Rolly's eyes shone as he pulled the moondial out of the front pocket.

"I thought I'd lost it forever."

"I suspected something like that might happen." Hranna nodded toward the front line of riders, who continued to move in a wedge toward the edge of the steep riverbank. The leader, dressed in blue, stuck out like a skisen horn. She then nodded back toward Rolly's own very interesting clothing. The skins looked good on him.

"I owe you, Hranna."

"I was your backup," she said. "I may not be a queen, but I have my moments."

Rolly's forehead creased. Hranna realized she might have gone too far. She'd wanted to hint that she knew about Rolly's situation. But she'd forgotten that his people didn't speak in circles like hers did. He might not catch the sympathetic undertones.

"Hello, Hranna." Inae picked a particularly inopportune moment to interrupt the conversation. Hranna looked over at the baggily-clad young man.

The consternation gathered around his eyebrows indicated that he'd known just how poorly he'd timed his greeting and had done so on purpose. Hranna remembered the feelings Inae had expressed for her previously. He must've taken a dim view of the reunion between her and Rolly.

She tried to give him a smile. "Thanks for not blabbing, Inae." Hranna could tell that he was rethinking that stratagem.

"What did you tell them?" she asked.

"The truth. That you'd convinced us we'd get rich trading with the strangers. We joined you. A hrall killed Anarra and Amrak in a freak accident. I quit and returned to the village, which is when I ran into this bunch."

"Thanks."

"Inoah called me a frostling."

"Well, you sort of are." Hranna couldn't help the jibe. She was so used to teasing him.

"Don't be so hard on the boy," said Balras, throwing his weight into the conversation. "It's not everybody who can lose a sled their first day on the ice."

"A hrall ate it!" Inae complained.

But they were all smiling at Balras's good humor; even Inae stopped pouting. She'd seen him for so long as a little brother. Hranna realized she'd have to be careful not to alienate him. She needed all the friends she could get.

"A hrall did eat it, just as Inae was rushing back to save me after I'd been thrown off my own sled."

Inae shot her an appreciative glance.

"Hranna thrown off a sled?" Balras laughed. "She's less sure footed these days."

Hranna took the awful pun in stride, "It was your stool that broke, but how can you expect an old bachelor to remember how to use wood."

Inae laughed. Yansil tittered. Rolly looked confused. As for Balras, he pulled a face, but even his frown betrayed him at the edges. He'd grown too used to smiling to bend his mouth entirely down. It rebounded into its usual state. Finally, he laughed, deeply from his belly.

"As sharp a wit as her father. I always said—" He realized his mistake too late. Balras glanced sharply at Hranna. Everyone else grew quiet.

She did not let her emotions show. "Tell me how he died, Balras."

"Inoah said he died in the fire."

"You were the first to the tent. Did you see his body?"

"No."

Yansil's trembling high voice intervened. "Ask that old fraud of a waterwan. He can talk to your father's spirit. I'll bet he won't."

"My father wasn't in the tent," said Hranna.

Balras looked genuinely surprised. "How do you know?"

"Because I started the fire."

No one spoke for a long time.

"Care to tell me what's going on?" said Rolly finally. "It feels like I slept through some important parts of this story."

Balras was no longer smiling. The look of grief on the face of her father's happy friend was a terrible sight to behold. "Hranna has just told us that Inoah murdered her father."

Yansil muttered, "Or had him murdered." Her voice trailed off, but Hranna thought she heard Yanka's name roundly cursed.

"And, Rolly," Hranna added, her face an immovable mask of metal that not even Toole's torch could bend, "Inoah has the same fate in mind for you and your people."

She did not add that her name was also on that list.

Chapter 17

The sun had woven behind the dark hull of the stranded vessel, casting a shadow on the group of sleds as they approached. It was the first darkness Hranna had felt since the moon disappeared nearly two ten-days ago. The open mouth of the shadow ate each sled in sequence as they rode before her. She and her group of Inae, Balras, and Yansil had been left in the rear. A frostling, an old man and woman, and a cripple, hardly of consequence to the warriors around them. They had been left to their own devices, even having to haul their own sleds down the riverbank unassisted.

On the shining, silver sled, Hranna had ridden easily to the bottom, cradling Yansil in her arms. They passed Inoah as he and Yanka carried the lead sled to the base of the ice floes. The look in Inoah's eyes would have frightened any of the others.

Yanka and Yansil locked stares the way a pair of male skisen might lock horns.

Hranna was beyond fear on Inoah's account. What could he do, kill her? No, he would not do that so long as he needed Rolly's cooperation.

That Inoah had given Hranna free access to speak with Rolly troubled her. Inoah must have thought Rolly lacked speech or that there was nothing Hranna could say that would change anything. Perhaps he was not counting on Rolly's willing cooperation at all.

During the ride to the cliff, she'd made it clear to Rolly that she expected treachery. The seasoned world explorer was hardly surprised. After all, he'd already had to barter his clothes to avoid losing his skin.

As she rode into the shadow of the boat, she wondered once again what the new chief had in mind. She tried to think how her father would have handled this situation. But it was without precedent in her mind. She would have to wait and see how events unfolded, just like everyone else, though not everyone else had a metal tube capable of shooting stars. If Inoah moved to harm Rolly, she would bring the heavens down on his sorry, blue hide.

The secondary group had already clustered behind the line of warriors, and a weak-looking Yanka. This time, Rolly's sled was among the leaders, right beside Inoah's.

From the side of the boat appeared several white faces along with one tanned like theirs and one unnaturally dark, scarred face. Hranna almost waved at them but stopped herself, considering the seriousness of the situation and how her own appearance with the band might seem to the people on the boat. Maybe they thought she was with them. She hoped Amy knew better.

Cupping a hand to her injured ear, she strained to hear what Inoah was saying to Rolly. As it turned out, the gesture was unnecessary. Rolly replied to Inoah in broken speech.

"Me no speak good. Her say good talk," pointing up at the faces peeking out over the side of the boat.

Oh good, smart, clever man, thought Hranna. If that was how he'd spoken to Inoah before, not only might the chief be unaware of Rolly's knowledge of their language, he might think him stupid as well. As Hranna knew from experience, it's hard not to feel stupid when you don't speak someone's language and harder not to think of someone as stupid who doesn't speak yours.

Inoah shouted up to the deck. "Your man told us of your troubles. We have come to help. We have luftall meat."

An uncomfortable feeling ran across Hranna's midsection. Inoah had begun the bargaining without hunkering down. Practically speaking, it made no sense to do so. His counterparts towered over them. It just felt wrong somehow, as if a bargain could be spoiled by the way it was made. Hranna shrugged away the thought as pure superstition.

The disembodied heads above deck moved closer together as Amy translated the message. Hranna thought she heard Toole's grating tone and Amy's sharp rebuke. She could see Toole shrug.

"You wear his clothing. Is he safe?"

"We exchanged clothing as a gift. He is standing beside me even now." Inoah slapped a hand across Rolly's back. "Now, what about an exchange?"

Hranna wondered if Amy caught the subtle meaning behind the words. She'd tried to explain to the enthusiastic doctor how different their two cultures were. A primary example was the way they communicated, with the blue-clad foreigners being very direct, save for Neko, while her people were so circumspect as to be obtuse.

After a brief consult, Amy replied, "We have meat enough already."

Hranna was certain that was not what Amy had wanted to say. She was taking her talking points from Toole, under protest, maybe, but she was speaking with his voice all the same. Unlike the previous day in the galley when Toole's word had been her death sentence, Hranna was glad that the voice of reason was being followed. Toole would handle things practically for the benefit of the crew and hopefully for Rolly, whose life, Inoah had just obliquely threatened.

Inoah continued, "As you say, but browen meat is nothing compared to luftall. Ask your friend."

Amy responded. "It is a bit tough. One moment, then." Amy switched over to their native language and interrogated Rolly.

Rolly responded in the foreign tongue.

Hranna noticed the impatient movement of Inoah's hands, which he held behind his back. He was not at all happy about being cut out of the conversation, and for good reason, thought Hranna. Rolly could very well be telling the strangers to rain fire down on the simple villagers. It was just another example in a long progression of Inoah's inexperience.

The conversation between Amy and Rolly was brief. Too brief, thought Hranna, to convey any really important information.

Amy returned her attention to Inoah, "He says that luftall meat is superior and that the fat has many uses. What is your offer?"

The fact that the boat was built entirely out of metal could not have escaped Inoah's notice. Yet his bid was almost circumspect.

"Equal weight: metal for luftall. As much as one sled can carry." Inoah gestured to a nearby rig pulled by two, big male skisen. It was loaded with luftall meat, probably from the very same beast Rolly himself had killed. If Rolly appreciated the irony, his body language didn't show it.

Again, the heads above deck bent together. Eventually, the reply came. Hranna was sure that Toole had belabored the discussion on purpose following in the ancient negotiating tactic of making the other party wait.

"We have use for each piece of our metal, but some may be spared. We will need time."

"Of course," said Inoah. "Also, please remember how we took such good care of your companion, even providing him a sled to ride on. We could not allow his sled to return empty. It would be bad luck."

That was a pretty subtle ransom threat, thought Hranna. She wondered if Amy understood the implications behind it. Inoah was saying that Rolly would only be returned alive for a price.

The meeting of minds on board ship lasted even longer this time. Toole's voice was never the loudest, yet it cut through all the others. Rolly must be able to hear what the man was saying. Maybe Toole was arguing that they couldn't spare the extra metal, just like they couldn't spare any food for Hranna. Maybe he'd grown used to running things. If he was really like Inoah, then Toole might see this as an excellent opportunity to get rid of his competition.

No matter what happened, it would be a banner year for the village. They would become the richest village on the wastes, for all the good it would do them with so little worth buying. They might use the metal for tools or also for weapons. Her hand shifted to the knife and her thoughts to her father. She wished she'd disturbed him that last day in the village, just to say goodbye.

Hranna considered for the briefest moment whether she might stick that knife into Inoah's back while he was distracted. If Toole was planning on selling Rolly out, such a risky move might save both her and him. Or just him. The others would probably fall on her, but maybe she would get the chance to explain, to plead her case about what Inoah had done to her father.

Actually, the idea felt nearly as good as the knife handle under her new blue gloves. Inoah had made her feel powerless again. She could take back the initiative. Given the fate awaiting her once the party left the shadow of the boat, what more did she have to lose? There was the red star, thought Hranna, tucked inside her blue backpack. But she had seen it bounce ineffectually off of the browen. This needed to be up close and personal, just like killing a luftall—get past its tusks to the meaty neck.

Hranna checked the movement of the knife out of its sheath. It slid smoothly up and down. She gathered up her crutch. It was a shame that she had only one foot. The crutch lessened her chances of sneaking up undetected. But if she walked casually enough, maybe the others would think she was only going to consult with Inoah.

Surely no one would suspect her true purpose, not even her friends, who might be trusted to keep their mouths shut anyway.

Hranna could hear the group arguing overhead. Toole's voice cut over them like a sled over ice. Whatever he said would win out in the end. Maybe Rolly could handle the man, but Rolly was down here, and no one up there had the courage to stand against him. They'd sent Hranna out to her death, after all.

With the carved luftall tusk held securely in her gloved hand, Hranna stepped off the silver sled.

Chapter 18

The debate on board ship lasted a few moments. Enough for Hranna to close the distance with Inoah's sled. Finally, Amy said, "We thank you and will, of course, repay the kindness you showed our companion."

Just a few more steps separated Hranna from the lead sled. Everyone was looking up. No one was paying her any attention, or if they were, didn't think her little walk worth mention. She breathed a sigh of relief at Amy's response. So, no matter what happened with her right now, Rolly would be safe. Toole had decided not to betray him. She wondered how close the vote had been.

Well, she had set off from the boat in order to save Rolly if she could. Who knew it would only take one day?

Now it was time to take care of herself. She put her hand to the hilt ready to draw the knife at the last possible moment. Yanka stood stupidly beside Inoah staring up as though he were speaking to the strangers' god in the sky. Bet he wished he'd predicted what she was about to do, thought Hranna.

She wasn't sure she could kill Inoah with the knife. A skisen horn would have been better, but definitely more noticeable. Whatever happened, she'd at least get one shot. After that, she'd put up her best fight. And if the other hunters descended on her, that was just one more story to tell of Hranna the Vengeance, who killed the man who murdered her father.

Their acceptance of Inoah's offer should have concluded the bargaining. Hranna needed to move quickly before the moment passed.

Hranna pulled out the knife and held it by her leg.

Amy called out, "We also want Rranna."

Hranna paused with her hand on the hilt of her father's knife, and the knife unsheathed at her side, at the edge of Inoah's sled. Just another step more and it would all have been over. Now she could not will her limbs to move. All eyes were fixed on her. Hranna froze, feeling as ancient a fixture on the ice as any glacial mountain.

"We need a guide to this frozen land. The hunter called Rranna."

If Inoah noticed her behind him, he did not show it. He ignored Yanka's feeble gestures in her direction and his warning about the knife.

Inoah spoke, with a tone of bitter resignation in his voice, "Hranna will be missed." He finally looked back at her as one might look at a beloved daughter; his eyes moved down her side to the knife, which glittered in the sunlight. His eyes narrowed. It almost looked like appreciation, as though he didn't think her capable of murder and was surprised and pleased to learn that she was.

"The pain of losing her would be less were we able to keep her sled. To remember her."

Amy called out to her. "Rranna, do you agree?"

She considered her answer carefully. It would mean leaving the village forever, which was not so great a concern with the bitter murder of her father and the threat hanging over her own head. But she had to accept in a way that would not cause Inoah to reconsider his offer.

"All that I have is for the good of the village," she said. "But these two skisen are my only family now. I could not part with them."

Inoah interrupted before Amy could speak. "Nor should you. We will trade your sled for the one the blue man rides. You will have your skisen and a sled for them to pull."

She considered asking for Inae's sled, the one Balras had built for her. But considering how she'd ruined his other sled, he deserved that one. And besides, she might talk Neko into designing her another one. Now that she knew what he was capable of, she had some suggestions.

Hranna looked round at her companions waiting behind her on the ice. They had been an unexpected source of support during the past fateful day.

Under the baggy hood, Inae bore a look of heart-ache so palpable Hranna almost laughed. It was hard not teasing him the way she once had.

Balras gave her a curt nod. His approval mattered strangely to her, knowing that her father was now dead.

Yansil, bundled in furs on the back of Balras's enormous sled, seemed not to be paying attention to the proceedings and might even have been asleep.

They would all return to their normal lives in the village. Inae to his mother Gyurtuh. He would find another love.

Nothing about this experience could make Yansil's life much worse or much better, though she would be bitter now that Yanka was of such importance to the new chief.

Hranna did worry about Balras though. The old man had just discovered that his best friend had been murdered. He had just seen what Hranna had planned for the murderer. He might feel duty bound to try to avenge her father. She hoped he would be smarter than she'd been about the whole thing.

"I accept your offer," she called up to Amy. Hranna would join the blue strangers. Indeed her legend would grow even more with the telling of how she boarded the boat made out of metal and sailed away to adventure with the strangers, even though the boat was clearly iced in and not going anywhere. Literalism killed sagas and was dispensed with liberally.

The import of the agreement struck her forcefully. Hranna was going to survive after all. She was going to live with the strangers and see their metal village. She would stay near Rolly. All her problems were over. The suddenness of it was enough to make her want to dance, to skip around like the girl that she almost still was.

As though he had sensed her thoughts, Inoah leaned toward her; yet, his sled did not move. His skisen were well trained, thought Hranna, as she readied the knife for whatever might follow.

Inoah whispered, "It's not over, Hranna." He indicated the boat with a nod of his head. "You can't stay up there forever. I want you to know it's not over." He paused, looking over the whole of the boat like a woman looks at a new tent. "I'll be seeing you soon."

A quick glance at Rolly indicated that he hadn't heard the threat. He had stepped to the other side of his sled and was busy unpacking supplies and unhitching his skisen.

By the snarl in his already low voice, Inoah had meant to intimidate Hranna. But he couldn't physically hurt her now, she realized, not without spoiling his bargain. So Hranna said the first thing that came to mind. "Suck a luftall intestine, Inoah. Suck it inside out. You killed my father, you frostling chief. You'd better pray to the ocean that you never see me again."

She turned on her heel and stumped back toward the silver sled, the beautiful contraption that had been hers for so short a time.

That felt good. But even as she'd said the words, Hranna realized the futility of trying to avoid fate. She and Inoah were destined to meet again. She didn't know whether to be excited or frightened by their inevitable confrontation. Regardless, she intended to be prepared.

Chapter 19

The moon stuck a silver tongue over the roof of the world. Hranna watched it rise with a sense of satisfaction and anticipation that she had not known since she was a girl. It always came back as a moon fully formed, no small sliver of light. It illumined the ice floes all the way to the river's edge nearly as bright as the sun.

Back at the village, they would be preparing the fire for the first gathering of the year. It was a time of great celebration. The impossibly thin Strau would bring the best of the luftall out of the village stores. Hranna could almost taste the crunch of the salty luftall fat roasted over a fire. Yansil would be peddling her teas. Meanwhile, those who reduced the fat to its spirits would be filling flagons with the potent draught. Visions would be seen tonight and babies made. Inoah and Hrite would wed tonight. To think that all of this might be happening only a short ride away was almost too much to bear. That life was closed to her forever. Like the moon, she must hide her face from the village for a time, for as long as Inoah ruled, perhaps.

Her only consolation was that someone else at least was not enjoying the gathering. Inoah must have left someone to watch over the vessel to send warning if they ever ventured out of the safe metal walls. Confident in his ability to track the group, Inoah would let them move away from possible retreat before striking. It's what her father would have done.

Yet, despite her warnings, the crew was preparing to disembark, to make their way to the metal village to the north.

The final whispered threat had been lost on Rolly, and Toole—though usually the practical one—had been as anxious as anyone to exchange the confines of the vessel for the confines of a series of metal tents. He had his work to do. She could appreciate that. It was almost physically painful for Hranna to be cooped up in a tent during a storm when she might be hunting on the ice.

Even now, as she leaned over the edge of the boat, her elbows secured against the frost of the metal railings by a layer of soft blue fabric, Hranna was watching for luftall signs under the ice. They'd be easier to see by day of course. But with a moon half as bright, an experienced hunter might be able to spot a slow moving beast.

Of course, Hranna was also on the lookout for the oversized shadow of a hrall. She'd thought she had caught sight of one just the other day, when Horkin was again paying obeisance to his gods. The entire metal frame of the boat had rattled with his deep, sonorous moans, as if the boat itself were praying along with him.

Tomas and Cynthia had complained during the afternoon meal in the galley, secure in the knowledge that Horkin would not be there to defend himself. He did not break fast during his days of prayer. Hranna wanted to respond that the tone was almost soothing and was in no way unpleasant, but she could not do so directly without having Amy translate, and she hadn't wanted to put her friend in the middle of an argument that there was no way of winning and no point in having.

Cynthia had been even colder to Hranna, were that even possible, since Rolly's arrival. Hranna could tell that Amy wanted to say something but was constantly having to check herself. Perhaps it had something to do with one of the secrets she kept for Rolly.

As for Tomas and Cynthia's complaints about Horkin, Hranna decided not to intervene in what must be as long running an issue as Yansil's feud with Yanka. They had endured life with Horkin on the vessel for some time. Perhaps they too had been intrigued by his piety at first, though she couldn't see how anyone could grow tired of hearing the low, melodious prayer wafting up from the big room, through the echoing gray corridors and into the air of the wastes. On seeing the shadow of the hrall during Horkin's prayer,

Hranna had begun to suspect that the black faced man was more of a waterwan than Yanka would ever be.

"Enjoying your new clothes?"

Rolly had snuck up behind her on the deck of the ship. That was uncomfortably easy to do these days. Hranna's ears were tuned for ice and snow. She could not get used to the wooden ground above deck or the metal floors below. With her new crutch that Neko built, Hranna wasn't sneaking up on anyone. The knock of her crutch against the ribs of the ship as she walked sounded, to her, almost at noisesome as Horkin's prayers down below, which had ceased as soon as the moon showed its face.

"Amy was kind to loan them to me. I can't believe your people have so many pairs of clothing. You must be so rich." Amy's clothes were a bit big on Hranna, but the feel of them was heavenly on her skin, like rolling around in a pile of snow that wasn't at all cold. In truth, she probably looked as floppy as Inae. She didn't care. Plus, they matched the fancy blue pack she'd been given and which she'd refused to give over to Inoah with the precious sled.

"That was quite a performance from Horkin today. I think he meant to impress you or maybe to convert you to his faith," said Rolly. His smile faded. Rolly must have noticed her pensive mood. "I must be very poor at jokes, I've made you sad."

"I was thinking about the gathering."

"Ah."

"The men will cook a whole luftall tonight. The oil as it seeps across the ice will burn without melting the snow, forming a great glowing circle of blue and gold flames. The women will dance."

"Amy is dying to see it."

Amy would die if she saw it, thought Hranna, and any of the others too. Inoah would see to that.

"I'm sorry my crew kicked you off the boat, Hranna. That was—"

"It was necessary," she said. "My problem. Not theirs."

Rolly shrugged, nodding his head to what she said, but his expression did not agree with the sentiment. She appreciated that at least.

"Hrolly, what is not necessary is for you to cross the ice."

He stood next to her, his hand on the rails, his elbows locked straight. A ten-day had done him good by way of recovery. He showed less pain when he moved.

The same could be said for her. Hranna had gotten used to the crutch Neko built. She had come to rely on the way its thin metal end bent and sprung back into place like a joint. She wondered if there were a way to skip the crutch altogether and simply attach the springy bit to the bottom of her leg. Hranna the Silverfoot, she thought. Yet none of her villagers would sing of that legend because they would never see it.

"We've talked about it, as you know. We simply can't stay here. Practically, we will eventually run out of food. And," he held up a hand to forestall her objection, "even if you hunt, there is the problem that the job that we came here to do is out there on the wastes."

Hranna tried to reason with him. "You say you have weapons. Single weapons like the red star. But Inoah has numbers. The number of hunters he brought before was strategic, few enough to show power and not so many as to intimidate you. He could call a hundred more to war, especially for so rich a prize."

"Our metal."

"Yes," said Hranna. She thought of a new tactic, "And what will happen to this ship if you leave? How will you return to your people? Won't Inoah take it while you're gone?"

"We dropped anchor as we were getting iced in." Rolly must have seen the confusion on Hranna's face as he added, "I mean the boat will stay here. And Toole thinks we can seal it up tight enough that no curious villagers can get at it with their primitive tools."

Hranna's face flushed, "We are not so primitive."

"I know," he backtracked, "but your bone tools are and your metal is not as strong as ours. Actually, that might be the funniest joke yet. Toole thinks that your people won't even be able to use the metal we gave them in return for the luftall. He thinks they won't be able to get it hot enough to melt."

The crew had stripped the boat of all the scrap metal they could find in order to pay what was essentially a ransom for Rolly and Hranna.

Apparently, Hranna had been saved at Toole's insistence. Maybe he thought Rolly would risk all their lives trying to save Hranna. Or maybe he thought they could spare some food for her now that they'd traded for the luftall meat. There had to be some kind of practical motivation behind the Toole's action.

To pay the debt, they'd had to sacrifice some of the inner doors to make weight. Toole had complained that if the boat took a beating or sprung a leak, they were going to miss not being able to seal those doors. Hranna had never known a vessel that could take a hole and yet keep floating. Toole had patiently explained why an empty cup floated on water but a full one sank; yet if three bowls were lashed together and one of them filled, the other two might keep the third afloat. It had been a terribly technical lecture, but Hranna had enjoyed it nevertheless, even though she hadn't understood half of it. Toole had even referenced one of the books in the library before realizing that Hranna could not read.

Amy had spent the last ten-day trying to rectify Hranna's ignorance in that regard. She had made fast progress, learning some of the scratches that made sounds on the paper and had learned some of their words by hearing. Still, she was a long ride away from reading one of those great books, or from sneaking a peek into Rolly's personal journal to see what he'd written about her.

It pained her a bit to think that her people really were primitive compared to Rolly and his crew. And though the small revenge of giving Inoah unworkable metal felt like justice, it was bittersweet, considering that it was the village that would suffer the loss of the traded meat and the greatest disappointment at the unusable metal. Inoah had the silver sled and would likely keep for himself whatever metal was pliable enough for the village metalworkers to shape. At least he might make a nice necklace for her friend, Hrite, and that thought comforted Hranna.

Rolly exhaled a big breath of visible air. "Let's get some sleep. Tomorrow's going to be a big day."

Yes, thought Hranna, it certainly would be. She would be back on the ice, a thought which cheered her. But Inoah was on the ice too. He'd threatened to kill her and the strangers, thinking them a threat to the survival of the village. He might suffer from deficient foresight, thought Hranna, but he was at least a man of his word.

Hranna gave a nod to the moon before turning to follow Rolly. When you go back into the ocean tonight, she said to the moon, I hope you will tell my mother and father what transpires and ask them for help. They would need it desperately if they were to make it to the metal village.

Hranna followed Rolly into the boat. He shut and barred the door behind them.

***

They walked through the darkened hallways together in silence—except for the tapping of her crutch which made her feel awkward enough to touch a hand to her ear. She'd been aware of the gesture before but had taken greater care ever since Amy called her out on it.

As they passed the galley, Hranna noticed that the light was still on and there were low voices coming from inside. The politician in her grew immediately tense, sensing a coup in the muted whispers. Rolly seemed nonplussed. Hranna tried to stifle the clack of her crutch but could not fully hide it. She heard a series of shushes issuing from the room. A coup for sure then. Toole may have taken Rolly on board, but he was obviously still planning to undermine Rolly's authority. Hranna quietly unsheathed her knife. Toole had sent her to die on the ice. It was clear whose side she was on.

"Hey, what have we here?" Rolly must finally have noticed the light. He walked into the room. Hranna waited a step behind, ready to spring into action.

The room went dark. Rolly did not cry out, nor did she hear a struggle.

Hranna hopped on one foot to the entrance. She could not let Rolly face the danger alone.

Hranna jumped into the room, her crutch held in front of her and her knife at the ready.

"Surprise!" the group shouted, but immediately fell into an awkward silence.

They were standing around the galley. A piece of roast luftall lay in a platter at the center of the table. The light in the room had been extinguished to better display a circle of flaming luftall oil surrounding the roast.

Hranna stared, uncomprehending, at the spectacle.

Amy spoke up, "We wanted to make a gathering."

The look on her friend's face shifted as mirth replaced the fright Hranna's entrance must have given her.

"We wanted to surprise you," said Rolly. "It looks like you surprised us too."

He translated his joke for the group. They chuckled appreciatively, the way one must when the leader tries to be funny.

Sheathing her knife and replacing the crutch under her arm, Hranna addressed the group with a broad smile. "Thank you," she said, and she said it in their language.

"Hear, hear!" called Jerome and, with that blessing, a small, mostly sober party—Rolly wouldn't let Toole convert all of the luftall fat into spirits, just some— commenced.

***

A small rapping noise brought Hranna awake. In her stupor, she checked to see if the crutch was by the bed or if someone was off playing around with it in the hallways causing the noise. The crutch was where it was supposed to be. The touch of cold metal against her hand brought Hranna wider awake.

She heard the tapping sound again. It was not a dream, then. Hranna rolled out of bed still fully dressed as was her habit. She couldn't understand what luxurious form of living the strangers must have enjoyed in their green lands that would allow them to feel comfortable sleeping naked. A cold enough sleep on the wastes and one might never wake up.

The room was dark, something she was still growing used to, it having previously been lit by the eternal sun of the moonless sky. Now the moon had returned and darkness with it, though the light from the moon itself was bright enough to navigate the room and narrow corridors. Besides, Hranna still didn't feel entirely comfortable lighting the wall fires as she called them. Amy had explained that the lights worked similar to the torch she had seen, sending an invisible cloud like the spirit of the luftall oil up a series of bladders or tubes to her room. She might open the bladder in her room and light the end, causing a small fire to illuminate the room. It was simply a wonder beyond what she was ready to contend with just now.

A shadow moved in the corridor ahead of her. Another of the crew might have called out to see who was there. Hranna's instincts ran to stealth and secrecy. Apparently the shadow's did as well since the person who cast it never bothered to greet her despite the rhythmic clanking of her crutch.

The weak rapping continued to come at even intervals.

Finally, at the stair leading up to the next deck, the shadow turned. Hranna was looking into a pair of white eyes that most definitely belonged to Horkin. The eyes moved down. He was nodding to her, acknowledging her presence. His head cocked up at the next series of knocks. She could tell he was pointing up. Hranna followed him up a series of stairs, pausing at every level to listen for the knock before proceeding higher.

In this way they came to the top level and to the door to the deck, the one Rolly had locked earlier that night. Standing in front of the door was the portly figure of Tomas.

Hranna wanted to ask him what he meant by knocking, but she lacked the words in their language.

Suddenly the rapping started up again, much louder this time because of their proximity to it. Hranna saw it was not Tomas knocking. Rather, as she should have suspected all along, the noise came from the other side of the door.

She wondered why Tomas had not opened it. The fat man himself raised his hands in a questioning gesture toward Horkin. Hranna realized the man had been afraid to confront what lay behind the door by himself. And perhaps for good reason, she answered herself. What if it was a trap set by Inoah and Tomas had let in a war party. The crew would have all died in their beds.

Deferring to Horkin, Tomas stepped out of the way as much as his fat torso would allow, and let the black man pass by.

Horkin put his hand to his belt, drawing out what looked like a sturdy, thin log. With the other hand he began slowly raising the bar on the door.

Hranna took out her knife. Tomas had somehow slithered behind her without her knowing it. The big man could sneak when he wanted to.

The door swung out onto the deck, knocking into someone who issued a yelp muffled by the heavy metal door. Horkin advanced onto the deck shutting the door behind him. Hranna just managed to squeeze out before it closed. She heard the bar drop behind her. Thanks for the help, Tomas, she thought.

In the waning moonlight of the last hours of the night, a figure lay seated on the wooden deck. He was a mass of fur clothing, obviously from the village, but not bearing a weapon.

Horkin replaced the wooden log in his belt and helped the visitor to his feet. Hranna knew at once who the tall, gangly form buried in furs must be.

"Inae?"

The young man threw back the floppy hood, revealing the long angles of his cheeks and nose. Horkin clapped him on the shoulder. The two had apparently hit it off during Inae's short visit to the boat some ten-day ago.

"What are you—?"

"You're in great danger. All of you," said Inae. "We came back to warn you—"

"We?"

"That Inoah has called out a war party. The whole village is coming."

"We?" Hranna repeated.

Sticking his thumb over his shoulder, Inae motioned toward the side of the boat, "Me and Yansil."

Oh no, thought Hranna, this is not happening. She moved over to the side of the boat to look down onto the ice below.

"And Balras," said Inae.

"Why aren't you at the gathering? Weren't you missed?"

"There was no celebration. Inoah canceled it."

Hranna couldn't even imagine why the villagers would agree to such a thing. Couldn't she, though? Inoah had brought back two sleds full of metal and one sled made entirely of the stuff, unbendable and eternal by their standards. He'd also probably told them about the giant boat made entirely of metal. It wouldn't have been hard to convince a few key hunters, and after they agreed, who would want to stay home? The fishers were no doubt eager to join up as well to avoid getting cut out of the deal. Who among them wouldn't want to see a metal boat?

No celebration? It was unheard of. And what of poor Hrite and her marriage.

She'd no sooner thought it than the question escaped her lips, "Hrite?"

Inae's eyebrows lowered, throwing his face into shadow. "Married to the murderer."

"But how?" Oh poor Hrite, to be married without a gathering. The village might accept it of a chief, but Hranna was sure that the other women would talk. How hard it would be for her friend to endure the gossip and the insinuations and the talk of curses or ill luck.

"Inoah was afraid you would sneak out under the cover of darkness. Even now the war party is assembling behind the rocks on the riverside."

"They'll pour down on us as soon as we move."

Inae shrugged. Horkin was looking at the pair of them expectantly. Tomas, meanwhile, had still not removed the bar and probably wouldn't till morning if he had his way.

"That's foolish though," said Hranna, "He should wait till we're well away from the boat."

"He talks about how few there are on the boat and how many of us, and he says," Inae paused and swallowed.

He was hiding something, thought Hranna. "And he says what?"

The depth of Inae's emotional pain showed in the corners of his eyes. "He says how we must rescue Yaokim's daughter from the strangers and all the things they might do to you."

"Ugh," said Hranna, "but I went willingly."

"I know, but Inoah says how you sacrificed yourself for the good of the village, like from your last speech. But, in private, he talks about how you might not resist their advances like a woman has the right to do."

Inoah had twisted her words about giving him the silver sled into something to suit his purposes and had implied that she lacked virtue.

"Hranna, I don't think Inoah knows we're here. We weren't part of the war party."

"You, Yansil, and old Balras, I can't think why not."

"Stop teasing for a moment. We've got to get Yansil and Balras off the ice before Inoah sees them."

Hranna doubted the chief's eyes were so keen in the darkness. Still, unlike her, Inae was using his head for something other than jokes. Maybe the frostling was growing up.

"Right," said Hranna. "Move them to the other side of the boat, away from the riverside—"

Inae struck his head at the obvious suggestion.

"And I'll have Horkin see about getting them on board."

Hranna made hand signals to the big man. "Friends," she said in their language, though she was beginning to suspect that Horkin was no more born to the tongue than she was.

He nodded and set about working on the series of ropes and metal rings that would carry even the heaviest loads safely aboard.

Meanwhile, Hranna waited patiently and quietly in spite of Inae's chatter, for Balras the Skisen-talker and for Yansil's wrinkled face to appear at the side of the boat.

The moon was halfway sunk into the ocean already. She had asked it to tell the ocean to send help. If this was the help she was getting, she wondered whether the moon's mind hadn't disappeared while it had been away.

Chapter 20

"Can you see them now?" Rolly's strong arms encircled hers, helping aim the pair of metal tubes that she held to her eyes.

Hranna suddenly felt very unsure of wanting to see clearly should it mean Rolly would break physical contact. How long could she keep this ruse going? They were standing on the deck, looking out toward the riverbank with a pair of magical, metal eyes. Others were waiting their turn. As Rolly relaxed his grip on her arms, Hranna thought she could feel Inae's eyes boring a hole in her head as big as a skisen horn.

"I see them," she said, finally. "They're camped on the side of the river, a little ways away from where we came down. Maybe they mean to hit us when we stop to port our sleds up the slope?"

"I brought a potion!" said Yansil. She searched through her fur pockets.

Great, thought Hranna, how perfectly out of context. The old woman often spoke without reference to anything else going on at the moment. The only good thing about her presence was how crazy she was making Tomas in the kitchen.

"Thank you," said Rolly.

He was too kind.

Toole was standing on the other side of Hranna with his own pair of metal eyes, black tubes that let the user see farther than a bird. He spoke to Rolly in his usual, gruff manner. She sensed no deference in the man's tone. Her father would never have stood for such insubordination. Rolly didn't seem fazed by it. He grabbed Toole on the shoulder and gave a quick smile.

"Toole says that we have to fight them. We can't wait them out. And there are too many of them for us to take on the open ice, which," Rolly nodded his head before Hranna could speak, "is exactly what you have been saying all along."

Toole muttered again before lowering his metal eyes.

"He says congratulations on being right," Rolly smiled again before growing serious. "We could just stay on the boat and leave when the ice breaks up, provided our food lasts that long. But we have important work that won't wait. We've got to think of something."

"We could sneak by them," said Inae.

"They'll track us down," said Hranna. "If we could get into the glaciers we might be able to force them to fight in the narrow tunnels." She was thinking of the look on Anarra's face when he died.

"A good idea," said the ever-smiling Balras. "But we'll have to sneak right under their noses to get there. Even then, they might circle around on us, box us in, and wait for us to starve. You know, kill the wollen when it sticks its head out the hole?"

The old hunter was right, of course, but Hranna never flinched in the face of danger. On a hunt, she would find a way to improvise. She let go of her conscious effort to force a plan and simply let her mind roam over the ice. Too soon she was thinking of hunting instead of the critical situation at hand. She saw a luftall shadow pass under the ice. Her arm tensed as if she might spear it from atop the ship. The hunt was in her blood.

She was not alone. A larger shadow trailed the luftall, moving quickly, consuming the luftall's shadow.

"I've got an idea," said Hranna quietly. "We could pray."

"We should all pray," said Rolly.

"No, I mean, Horkin. We should ask him to really pray." She pointed at the disappearing shadow of the hrall under the ice.

"You don't really think—" Rolly began. No one on board really believed that Horkin had caused the attack that killed Amrak and destroyed Inae's sled. No one but Hranna and Horkin.

"It's worth a shot, don't you think?"

"Even if it did work, how would we get Inoah onto the ice?"

"Oh, I think he'll come if he sees his chance to kill me."

Hranna explained her plan. Rolly translated. As he listened, the sides of his mouth sank under a frozen sea of concern. He did not like her plan one bit. Toole, on the other hand, began nodding more and more. He saw the risk, thought Hranna, and he liked it.

***

"What do you mean you won't do it?" said Rolly. Amy stood next to Hranna, providing a contemporaneous translation of this battle of wills. Rolly's fist slammed against the table fixed to the floor of the galley. He hit it so hard Hranna thought she saw the pictures on the wall jiggle. Rolly's mood could not have been improved by the smell and by the low foggy haze pouring out of the kitchen filling up the galley's floor.

Yansil had been back at it that morning, much to Tomas's regret.

Horkin seemed unmoved by the display. "It is not the proper day."

"What do you mean, proper day?" said Rolly. "I don't think your gods will mind your praying a day or two early."

Horkin fixed him with a stare. "The gods of my people are not like yours. We do not ask them to take notice of us. We beg them to ignore us."

"Then your gods aren't very good."

"I never knew a god that was," said Horkin.

"Oh, wow." Amy added that last bit. Her translations often contained a sort of running commentary.

"Our god," began Jerome. The entire crew from the ship was gathered around the table. Balras and Inae joined them as well. Yansil. Well, Yansil was in the kitchen as anyone with a nose could tell.

"He was making a joke, Jer," Rolly interrupted. "He doesn't mean that."

"He might," said Toole.

"You'd like that, then, Mr. Ohanna," said Jerome, looking at Toole, "if our fellow crew member were going to hell?"

"Ah, let it go," said Cynthia.

"This isn't a theological debate," said Rolly. "We're all believers here, including Horkin, though he may not believe like we do."

"See where this ecumenicalism has gotten us?" said Jerome. "He refuses to help."

Hranna shook her head at that last line of translation. Amy tried again but had difficulty conveying the meaning. "Jerome says to worship all gods equally is to worship no god truly."

Hranna nodded. She thought the fussy man had a point, however impolitic his expression. She too was at a loss to understand why Horkin would not pray at this crucial time. Jerome might pray to the sky; Hranna had never stopped praying to the ocean, though it had sent her poor help so far in the form of a frostling, an old healer, and a man who thought he could talk to skisen. Why shouldn't Horkin pray too?

"I can pray," said Toole.

"You never—" Jerome said before catching himself. He ran a hand over his gray head. "What I mean to say is, it is hardly the same thing."

"So," said Toole, "you admit his prayers would be more effective than mine?" His smile was drawn back at the lips like a wollen's.

"That's not what I meant and you know it," said Jerome.

"Is that crazy old woman ever going to leave the kitchen?" said Tomas.

Everyone ignored him, including Toole. "Don't worry. I wasn't meaning to pray to your god anyway. I mean to pray to Horkin's."

Toole continued to smile, accepting all of Jerome's apoplectic rage.

Hranna tuned out the translation. She didn't understand many of the finer points that Jerome was making about religion. She thought about what Toole said, knowing that a man like him never said anything without reason.

"I will too," Hranna blurted out. "I'll pray too."

"Really?" Amy skipped a beat in her coverage of the great battle of religions.

"I'm not converting to his religion, Amy," Hranna said. "It's the sounds, right? We just need to make the sounds."

"Oh," said Amy and fell to describing Hranna's point to the rest of the team.

Toole nodded, as if to say, exactly. Jerome also looked satisfied if not entirely comfortable with the arrangement. Rolly beamed at her; Cynthia seethed. Basically, order had been restored.

"Toole, do you think you can do it?" said Rolly.

"If it's just a function of producing the right frequency of sound, sure. If he's actually talking to gods, not so much," he paused. "I think it will work. Why don't you ask our resident animal lover?"

Rolly turned toward Cynthia, "You're the biologist. What do you think?"

The blonde-haired woman composed herself with a smile meant just for Rolly. "We've long thought the animals of the ocean communicate to each other. But we've never been able to talk to them."

"Until now?" asked Rolly.

"Maybe." She sounded so feminine when she said it.

"Okay then. We go on with Hranna's plan," said Rolly.

The infuriatingly red smile on Cynthia's face disappeared like the sun behind a cloud.

Rolly barked out orders, "Neko, Horkin, and Toole, get into the hold and go to work. I'll join you soon as I've got Hranna, Inae, and Balras squared away."

He looked around the room with his nose in the air. "Tomas and Cynthia, do you think you could get Yansil out of the kitchen and get us some proper food prepared? No offense." He glanced at Hranna.

She was not about to defend Yansil's cooking.

"Okay, then we know what we need to do. We've got till tonight to do it. Pray to whatever gods you call on that it works."

Chapter 21

The full moon rose, as big white and round as a skisen's backside over the barren wintery landscape. Hranna held the moondial up to the night sky. She aligned a reticle on the open lid of the dial with the full moon. A small shadowy line fell over the face of the dial, pointing to one of the ornate carvings on the side. Taking a reading was so simple that a child, or a savage like her, could do it. Yet the moondial was the work of an entire civilization.

She closed the precious piece of metal and handed it back to Rolly, who was removing the far-seeing metal eyes from his.

"I can't see any fires," said Rolly.

"You can only travel by night?"

"What?"

"The moondial. You can only use it at night?"

"Nothing's perfect. The sun isn't constant enough to—"

"I mean, no offense, but it's kind of impractical—"

"It also has a compass."

Hranna raised an eyebrow.

"A pointy thing that points to the top of the world." He paused and, apparently not receiving the look of comprehension that he wanted, continued, "Tells you what direction you're heading?"

Hranna gave her best non-committal shrug.

She hadn't really expected Rolly to see any fires. Her people would not be so careless with their fuel. And, too, they must know that fires can be seen from such a long way away at night.

A part of Hranna felt bad for the men and women assigned to keep watch during a long, cold night without a fire. Another part of her hoped they might freeze a foot off—well, not a foot, it was hard living without a foot—but something that would prevent them from taking place in the raid. They were just following their new chief, but that did not make Hranna feel any better about the villagers' choice to aid Inoah. Only Inae, Balras, and Yansil had shown any type of decency or concern about killing innocent strangers.

"If you're going to do this thing," said Rolly, "then it's time."

Hranna rose up on her tiptoes, balancing on the one foot. She kissed Rolly lightly on the cheek.

"What was that for?"

"For in case I don't come back," said Hranna. "For being a good man."

"Well, I don't know about that," Rolly began.

"I do." Without another word, Hranna slipped over the side of the boat, sliding down one of the thick ropes to the ice below. Inae was waiting for her and Balras as well. She whistled for Bin and for Moon. The two beasts trotted along and were patient when hitched to the sled.

"Are you sure you don't want my team?" said Inae. "They're faster."

"They're faster in a short run," said Hranna, "which is all this will be, but even so, I don't fancy going against a hrall without Moon at my side. And Bin saved me from the browen." It seemed ages since the brave skisen had stuck her horn straight into the browen's exposed flank.

"Can't we come with you?" said Balras. "What would your father say if he knew I let you face danger alone?"

"He would be proud of me for doing what needs to be done," said Hranna, though she knew it wasn't the truth. If she succeeded, many villagers might lose their lives tonight. They were hunters, true, and a hunter longs to die on the ice. Her father would never forgive her what might be viewed as a betrayal of the village.

Hranna fumed. What should she have done, submit to her own death? That didn't seem right either, especially since she longed so fervently to live.

That strong desire for life had led her out onto the ledge to battle the luftall and had pushed them forward when the browen hunted them. It had driven her to risk everything in a flight through the glaciers and across the ice. And now, it was that love of life that forced her to risk her own life for a chance to save it and others she loved.

It was her plan. She was still the best rider, even on one leg, and Inoah wanted her dead. So Hranna had volunteered to take the most risk.

Inae and Balras lit the torches on her sled and on the other two sleds waiting nearby. Afterward, they climbed hand-over-hand up the thick rope.

Hers was a new metal sled designed by Neko and Hranna. It wasn't as pretty as the first one they'd built. There wasn't enough time for detail work. Still, she was glad to have it for the coming adventure.

Hranna called to her skisen, Bin and Moon, to move out. As soon as they were a length away, she turned and gave hand signals to Inae's team and to Balras's skisen as well. The well-trained teams fell in line behind her. They came around the side of the boat carrying lit torches. Now, Inoah could see them as easily as Hranna had first spied the moondial.

***

Across the ice floes atop the frozen river, Hranna's three sleds cut across the thin ice that separated life from the watery grave of souls. Their runners ran silent and smooth. Their riders were as still as glaciers. Their leader gave silent signals to her team using hand signals.

Hranna was leading them directly toward the riverbank and, though she could no longer see them, the great glacial mountains. Hranna was heading straight for Inoah.

Looking behind her, she saw each of the sleds occupied by two riders, dressed in blue.

There was no one in the blue clothes. They were
the crew's old snow suits, patched many times over
and as holey as her tent. Still, they looked a great
sight better than tanned luftall and skisen hides that
her people wore. It would be a shame to waste them.
Rolly seemed to think he was avoiding a lot of trouble
having to wash them. Given the thorough job done
on her own skins when they'd been returned to her
on board ship, she couldn't blame him.

A dummy sat behind her as well, making their party six in all. Technically they should have been nine,
but she doubted Inoah was counting.

Hranna's attention returned to the ice in front of
her sled. Driving a rig in the dark could be a dangerous proposition even with the full moon and a lit
torch to guide you. And even if your sled was made of
the hardest metal.

Again, Hranna's luck betrayed her as the ultra white
landscape turned from gray to solid black. She looked
up in time to see a giant cloud swallow the moon. Her
bad luck demon was at work again. Or maybe Rolly's
people had not prayed hard enough to their god in
the sky. She hoped that their prayers to Horkin's dei-
ties might be more effective. All of their plans hinged
on it.

The snow rushed up in front of the sled. It was
amazing just how fast they seemed to be going when
she could only see a few steps ahead. She had to trust

her instincts and her skisen, Bin and Moon. Too bad Moon was also half-blind. Hranna strained to see every oncoming piece of ice as it rushed into view. Her eyes flickered like a flame in the wind, looking for any variation in the ground.

It was this intense concentration that saved her. Hranna noticed Bin's head raise ever so slightly. Normally, she wouldn't have thought much of such a small movement. Driving blind on the ice into the teeth of the enemy, though, Hranna was sensitive to any clues she could get about her surroundings.

Moon's rhythmic stride didn't reveal anything out of the ordinary. That was a good thing, for now.

The moon overhead wrestled with the clouds sending off sporadic bursts of light, painting white patches on the darkened landscape. In those bright pockets in the distance, shadows moved.

Bin grew even more restless. Hranna couldn't take any chances.

Hranna reached into the blue pack tied to the sled. The metal tube slid out. She pointed it into the sky. This wasn't according to plan, but she had to be able to see. A red star raced from her hand toward the cloudy moon. She reloaded almost as soon as she fired.

As the star rose, Hranna gasped. Sleds were pouring over the side of the steep riverside, moving like a pack of wollen on the hunt.

Hranna counted thirty sleds at least. The lead sled was already on the face of the river. Its metal frame glowed with a deep red shine. Its rider's now purple-looking clothes marked him as none other than Inoah, her father's killer.

Hranna called Bin and Moon to a stop. Blood flooded her face, making her ears ring. She stashed the metal tube and grabbed the hafted skisen horn from its place on her sled. They were finally going to meet. Inoah was going to die.

Moon's head shot up and her tail lashed the air. The movement saved Hranna's life. She'd been about to ride right into the heart of the enemy attack.

Now, she remembered the plan. The red star had been the signal. At the first sight of the red flame, deep in the heart of the boat, Toole would begin pumping away on his prayer machine, something both Horkin and Jerome equally regarded as an abomination.

Toole had connected a series of metal pipes that he was fairly certain would reproduce Horkin's warbling entreaties if enough air could be put through them. Toole had tried blowing and had almost passed out without getting so much as a toot to come out of his precious pipes. Finally, at Neko's suggestion, they'd rigged a series of bellows, great bladders that alternately filled with air then pushed air out. These must have worked.

Warned by Moon's growing alarm, Hranna put the plan into action. Her part was simple: run.

"Hyop! Hyop! Hall, Hall," Hranna called to Bin and Moon to make a tight turn. They heard the urgency in her voice and felt her foot leaning on the sled.

The red star hung in the air. Shadowy sleds came fast across the ice, on an angle to cut off her retreat. Hranna urged her team back to the boat. They needed no encouragement. The riderless sleds followed Hranna, drawn by skisen that looked as confused as Moon looked scared.

Hranna hadn't expected Inoah to attack so soon. She'd expected him to wait on the riverbank for her party to arrive, knowing they would have to dismount to move their sleds up the steep bank. Once Inoah made his move, she would lure him onto the ice.

Instead, he must have decided to take advantage of the cover the cloud had provided. He'd almost succeeded.

By the time Hranna got turned and up to speed, the lead sleds were only a few lengths away. It was going to be a race to the boat, similar to the one she and Amrak had run.

For once, she wished she'd taken Inae's offer of the male skisen team. With Bin and Moon in the lead, the sleds following her could only go as fast as Bin and Moon, which was plenty fast. But Inoah's skisen were faster. Hranna signaled to the teams. The first broke to the left. The second pair broke to the right at her command.

As the red star fell to toward the ground, the first of the war party took the bait, attacking the hindmost sleds. A skisen horn went into the back of one of the blue-clad dummies. A cry of triumph rose from the hunters as the blue-clothed figure slumped and fell off the sled.

Inoah didn't chase the other sleds. He was not looking for glory or the spoils of battle. He was looking for Hranna. As his strong team pulled alongside hers, Inoah lifted his hafted hunting horn, preparing to skewer her.

Moon skittered to the right. Hranna gave up control of the sled and let her skisen run. Inoah hadn't anticipated the sudden movement. He stabbed air.

Hranna gave him a curt nod as her sled pulled away. He yelled something after her. She couldn't hear what he said over the noise of exploding ice. A hrall punched into the air.

One of Inoah's riders disappeared into the gaping maw of the writhing hrall. Inoah was shouting again. She thought she might have a clue what he was saying this time, a bit of a prayer and a curse all at once. It seemed the hrall inspired that sort of prayer.

Moon pulled back to the left. In the patchy moonlight, Hranna saw a huge shadow pass under the ice. Behind them, the frozen river erupted again. A second hrall took out a pair of skisen, destroying the sled with its muscular back. What remained of the rider slid down the hrall's gray bulging sides, only to be crushed under the weight of the hrall when it hit the ice.

Two hrall! Oh great ocean, thought Hranna. Toole's plan was working maybe even better than they hoped.

She looked for Inoah. He was still in pursuit. Yanka was near him.

But Hranna's erratic driving had put Hranna in the path of another of his hunters, a female cousin on Inoah's side of the family. Hranna ducked just in time as a hunting horn swiped past her head. Hranna wanted to kick out, then remembered she was missing a foot, cursed fate, and reached for her knife.

As the first hrall fell back into the river and the second ground the bones of the hapless hunter under its thrashing flesh, a hole opened right in front of Hranna's sled. Moon and Bin jerked. She passed a hand's breath away from a grinding, multi-layered wall of hrall teeth. The stench of rotting fish filled its fetid mouth.

Her pursuer was not as lucky. She plunged head first into the mouth of the hrall. The hrall chewed her without moving a jaw, the sharp rows of teeth cutting the hunter into strips that slid down its slippery throat.

Hranna put the back of a hand to her mouth. She remembered dancing with the woman at the gathering. She hadn't deserved to die that way. Hranna struggled to remember if the hunter had children. If so, they were orphans now just as she'd been.

Hranna glanced over her shoulder. The last hrall was still on the ice. The other two had slipped back into the river. Inoah's hunters were scattering. One, its skisen running mad, plunged into one of the watery holes left by a hrall. He fell screaming into the icy water. His skisen were pulled under, still harnessed to the sinking sled. The rider would likely not survive the wetting.

Inoah was not entirely defeated. He'd rallied nearly a dozen riders, including Yanka. They were still giving chase but were having a difficult time following Hranna's erratic movement. She wasn't traveling in a straight line. Truth was, she wasn't even driving. Moon was doing all the work. Bin and Hranna and the dummy behind her were merely along for the ride.

Moon jogged to the right. Too late this time. Hranna felt the sled rising into air that was suddenly full of hrall teeth. Moving fast, Hranna cut the harness holding Bin and Moon. The pair raced on, still tied together, toward the black boat. She hoped they would live.

The momentum of the sled almost carried it out of the hrall's mouth. Sharp teeth bit down on the end of her sled and snapped it up into the air. Hranna held on for her life as the front of the sled turned vertical. The dummy, too, held fast, tied as it was to the sled.

The front of the sled continued moving in a slow arc, propelled by the beast's grip on the tail of the sled.

Hranna jerked hard, rolling in the air. The sled rolled with her, coming down runners-first on the rows of flashing teeth.

It was time to see if Neko's design on the new metal sled would work. Hranna closed her eyes.

The sled hit the first row of teeth. It scraped against the chassis, making a grinding sound. But the sled did not break.

Hranna looked past the runners, down into the open throat of the hrall. A torch fell from its mooring on her sled down, down into the cavernous belly. Undigested parts of hunters and skisen were illuminated by the falling torch.

The hrall closed its jaw, trying to crush the metal sled.

It bent but did not give. The hrall thrashed, trying to get a better grip. As it landed belly-down on the ice, Hranna grabbed her crutch and her pack and jumped. The dummy fell with her, apparently thinking, like her, that it would rather not get dragged down into the water when the hrall got tired of breaking its teeth on the sled.

Hranna had survived a hrall attack. But she was now sled-less and skisen-less. The hrall tossed aside her bent sled before collapsing back into the river. The sled skittered to a halt on the ice.

Immediately Hranna turned, looking for Inoah. He was looking for her too, riding toward her, her death in his hands.

Chapter 22

You had a good run, Hranna," said Inoah. He and ten other riders formed a semi-circle around her. They looked nervously from Inoah to the ice underneath their sleds. Another hrall attack would take out half of their company. Hranna was prepared to die with them. Yet the ice did not break.

The moon, still half-clouded, flickered across Inoah's grim face.

"The friends who rode with you are dead," he said. "Any who remained on the boat soon will be as well."

Hranna had heard enough. She would rather die now than listen to any more of his smug speech.

"There was no one in the sleds, oh great chief. Your people died for nothing." Hranna kicked at the blue-clothed dummy lying on the ice beside her. Instead of stuffing, her foot connected with a solid mass.

A smattering of curses escaped from the dummy. "Stop kicking me."

Hranna stared in amazement as a small head slid up the neck of the blue suit, filling the fur lined hood.

The wrinkled visage frightened Hranna worse than anything else that night.

"Yansil?"

The old woman winked at her.

"What are you doing here?"

"Wanted to teach that phony waterwan a lesson," said Yansil. "And I brought you a potion."

Yansil held one of Rolly's metal flagons, open, in her hands. The smell coming from the potion was palpable.

"No thanks."

"It's magic."

Hranna shook her head. Inoah's teeth were bright. He was obviously enjoying the show.

Yanka called out in a sharp voice, "Yansil, you old skisen, how did you get out here? Not on your own, I think? Any more traitors with you?"

Yansil gave Hranna a suit-yourself shrug before turning toward Yanka. "Waterwan, did your wet spirits tell you how this ends?"

"You will be able to ask them yourself soon enough."

Metal glinted in the moonlight as Yansil upended the flagon into her mouth. A wicked smile creased her already folded wrinkles.

The speed with which Yansil moved took Hranna's breath away. What had been a hobbling old body transformed into a blur of motion, flying across the ice as quick as a snow rabbit. In one mighty leap, Yansil hit Yanka in the shoulders, taking him with her, tumbling over his sled onto the ice. The potion must have been potent.

Inoah reacted nearly as quickly. "Get them!"

The riders dismounted and raced toward Hranna.

Her blue pack fell to the ground. In her hands was the metal tube. She took aim at Inoah. Her knife still held in her hand atop the tube, steadying the shot. Legs shoulder width apart, leaning slightly as though she was inching a team of skisen forward, she squeezed, just as Rolly had taught her. A flaming ball of red light scattered the hunters. Her hand bucked.

It took Inoah fully in the chest, carrying him over the back of his sled in a ball of fire.

Always have a backup, Rolly had said. Turned out he was right.

Hranna dropped the smoking tube and readied her knife. Neko had also given the bottom of her springy crutch a sharp edge. One of the hunters rushing toward her again was about to get a surprise.

She waited for them with a snarl on her face.

***

As the first of the hunters reached her, Hranna heard the sound of ice breaking behind her: a series of several pops, as though a sheet of ice was about to fall into the river.

The hunter stopped and looked down. So did Hranna. She expected to see row after row of hrall teeth churning through the ice. Nothing happened.

When Hranna looked up, the hunter was still looking at a stream of blood pouring down the front of his furs. He collapsed to his knees before falling onto his side on the ice, never to move again. Several hunters and a skisen fell with him. Other skisen teams fled at the sound. Chaos reigned.

Before Hranna could even speculate as to what had happened, a brace of blue uniforms rushed by either side of her, dropping smoking sticks as they passed. It was Horkin and Rolly. Moonlight glinted off of long metal knives in their hands. Balras and Inae holding skisen horns also raced past.

Tomas and Jerome stopped beside Hranna, still holding their sticks. They were of the same design as the one Horkin had pulled from his belt on the night of Inae's arrival.

Jerome fumbled with his.

"What's happening?" said Hranna.

"Reloading," he said. "We stopped the prayer when we saw you were in trouble. We came to—" A skisen horn took him through the chest, and his explanation died on his lips. A hunter had caught them unawares.

As Jerome fell, Hranna swung her crutch in an glittering arc across the ice. The sharpened edges sunk deep into the hunter's neck, getting stuck in his spine. His body crumpled, nearly taking her crutch with it. Struggling, she pulled it from his corpse.

Tomas pointed his stick into the night, backing up against Hranna. She understood what he meant to do and placed her back against his, raising her knife, keeping her crutch at the ready.

They circled, watching as hunters and strangers fought. Balras, dressed as a hunter, had taken his opponent by surprise and had pinned him to the ice by a horn, Balras's weight drove the man down onto the ice as though he were securing a tent pole.

Inae was kneeling beside a fallen body, a female warrior. He was clutching his right arm, his face a bloody mess.

Yanka and Yansil were nowhere to be seen.

Rolly and Horkin were trading blows with their long metal blades. The hunters defending with the skisen horns were driven back, inexperienced in this kind of battle. Horkin's blade sang through the air, snickering straight through the raised horn and into the man's skull. He flicked the blade back, not losing it in the victim as Hranna had done.

Almost simultaneously, Rolly's blade locked with his opponent's curved skisen horn. He twisted, sending the weapon out of the man's hands. A death blow did not follow. Rolly spoke. And the man sat down on the ice.

He had saved the life of one of her villagers. Rolly understood. In that moment, Hranna loved him.

A shout and a cracking shot came from behind. Tomas had fired his stick. Hranna turned in time to see Tomas swept aside by a mighty blow delivered by Inoah.

Inoah stood in front of Hranna with a bloody knife in his hand.

Tomas lay crumpled in the snow, a pool of blood forming where Inoah had sliced the man's stomach.

Inoah's blue uniform was charred black and stunk like burnt hair. His face was a mask of red blisters. Half of his lower lip and his right eye were missing. In his hand was a bloody knife. Death stared back from his eye as malevolent as the dark orb of a hrall.

There was no more talk. No smug speeches. No preliminaries.

Inoah raised his knife. Hranna held hers at the ready.

He rushed forward, same as a tired though deadly luftall aiming to skewer her with its fore tusk. This was a dance that Hranna knew well.

Pivoting on her good foot, she turned as he came in, moving toward rather than away from him. Avoiding the outstretched knife, Hranna closed with Inoah's body. He had no hind tusks to protect him. Her knife sliced through what was left of his neck. The skin crackled like a burnt luftall steak as she cut through.

She kept turning, stopping to face him. Inoah took two more steps before collapsing on the snow.

His throat gurgled. He was trying to say something.

"Tell it to my father." Hranna picked up her metal crutch and plunged the sharpened end into his back, aiming for his heart.

Chapter 23

Nearly a ten-day later, sunrise from the top of the boat still revealed a massive scene of carnage across the frozen river. Snowfall had not yet buried all evidence of the battle. Hranna adjusted her fingers in the blue gloves.

"Are you sure that you have to go?" said Rolly. He looked tired. Cleaning up after the fight had been hard work.

They had tended to the wounded. Tomas would survive. He'd been lucky to have such a fat stomach. Inoah's knife hadn't reached anything vital.

Inae too would recover, though it would be some time before he regained use of his arm, if ever. He claimed the scars on his face would make him look distinguished, older and perhaps more attractive.

Yansil had helped care for the injured villagers. Her opponent, Yanka, was not among them. Nor was his body discovered on the ice. Yansil would not say what had happened between her and the waterwan except a cryptic aside that he would have plenty of time to commune with the ocean.

Rolly had wanted to give the bodies of the dead villagers a proper burial till Hranna reminded him that a covering of snow was as proper for a hunter as any rite or ceremony. They left the dead where they fell except for Jerome who they honored by burning his body, sending it into the sky.

Sighing, Hranna finally responded to Rolly's question. Down below, she saw Inae and Balras preparing four sleds for the journey. There were two metal sleds now, hers and Inoah's, along with the custom sled Balras had made for Hranna and his own long sled.

"Their chief is dead," said Hranna. "The village is vulnerable. I have to help."

"Vulnerable because of you," said Rolly. "You sure they won't turn on you?"

Hranna considered carefully. It was a thought that had often occurred to her in the past few days. Some of the hunters must have survived and might have fled the deadly river back to the village carrying the story with them. Had any of them seen her kill Inoah? If so, would they have told his widow, Hrite? She had killed the husband of her best friend only a day after their wedding.

"It's a risk I'll have to take."

"And Amy?"

"She said she wants to come."

Rolly shifted his weight. Hranna had begun to be able to read his moods as easily as those of a close relative. He wasn't happy, but whether his dark mood was in response to Amy's traveling with them or something else, something concerning Hranna, she couldn't tell.

"You will come and see us? In our metal village?" said Rolly.

"When I can. I've got to bring Amy there, remember?"

"Then you'll need this." Rolly's hand fished in his front pocket. He removed a small metal object, holding it out to her.

This time it didn't fall to the ground as she reached for it.

"Your moondial?"

Hranna didn't know what to say. Rolly stared sheepishly at the wooden deck.

"You were saving this for your son."

"I still am," he said, looking at her with an intensity in his blue eyes. A breeze blew past him, carrying with it the scent of fresh cut trees. "You'll bring it back to me?"

To one born on the ice, to a people who spoke enigmatically, his meaning was perfectly clear. She reached for her knife, slid it out of its sheath, and pointed it at his chest.

"You know the women of our village can kill a man for talking like that?"

"Amy mentioned it."

Hranna brought her knife forward, but slowly. She flipped the edge into her palm, handing the carved tusk handle to Rolly.

"I was saving this for my son," she said.

"I'll be sure to take good care of it," he said, "for your son."

She leaned up, as she had that final desperate night, and kissed his cheek lightly before slipping over the edge of the boat. She slid down the thick rope to the frozen river below.

Moon and Bin came at her whistle. Over the past few days, Bin's belly had started to show. Not everything of Nar would disappear from the ice. Hranna hoped the baby skisen would be a male.

She hitched the pair to her sled, the one Inoah had taken from her. Amy would drive the other.

Hranna pointed the runners of the sled into the frozen wastes of the planet Hurt. The world was so much bigger than she'd ever imagined. Endless freedom stretched before her. She could go anywhere. Yet Hranna's duty lay, as ever, in the direction of her village.

ABOUT THE AUTHOR

Hans Hergot is the pen-name of an award-winning author of fantasy and science-fiction whose stories convey a redemptive message. He lives in the Republic of Korea with his wife and five children. Learn more at www.hanshergot.com.

Sign up for a (low volume) mailing list announcing new titles at http://tinyurl.com/hergotlist.

***

The original Hans Hergot lived nearly five hundred years ago. He was a writer, a pamphleteer, and a book seller who wandered from village to village bringing knowledge and truth. He was burned alive for speaking a wisdom that the world could not understand.

Deo vindice

www.ingramcontent.com/pod-product-compliance
Lightning Source LLC
Chambersburg PA
CBHW020236260626
47156CB00002B/696